Dazzle and Dance

by Stacy Davidowitz
Illustrations by Victoria Ying

AMULET BOOKS
NEW YORK

Cataloging-in-Publication Data has been applied for and may be obtained from the Library of Congress.

ISBN 978-1-4197-3129-7

HASBRO and its logo HANAZUKI and all related characters are trademarks of Hasbro and used with permission. © 2019 Hasbro. All rights reserved.
Book design by Pamela Notarantonio

Printed and bound in China
10 9 8 7 6 5 4 3 2 1

ABRAMS The Art of Books
195 Broadway, New York, NY 10007
abramsbooks.com

CONTENTS

you delicious purple monster. I dare you. Show me your courage!"

"Really, CP?" Hanazuki said. "You're encouraging this, too? We go through this every day, multiple times a day. It's all fun—well, partly fun—until someone gets hurt."

"I admit I have a love-hate relationship with this game."

"Self-awareness is a great start. Now let's unpack the 'love' part."

Just when Hanazuki thought she was getting somewhere, Purple Hemka kicked up some moon dust and raced into Chicken Plant's pouncing zone. He hopped forward from side to side, like he was playing a game of hopscotch. Chicken Plant pounced, just missing Purple's ear. She pounced again, just missing his other ear, and her beak got stuck in the ground. Her eyes bulged as she tried to squawk. The Hemka ran around in circles, screeching.

Hanazuki covered her ears. All this noise was

making her head pound. Why couldn't everyone take a chill pill? The Treasure Trees were healthy. The Big Bad was out of sight. No outside forces were threatening the moon. So why were her friends acting so crazy? Didn't they want a relaxing staycation? Didn't they know they could be reclining on moon-rock chairs, cucumbers on their eyes, soaking in the sun? Didn't they know that drinking fruit juice by the lake was all the rage? *It's called 'life choices,' creatures!*

Soon enough, Dazzlessence Jones and Sleepy Unicorn arrived on the scene. "*Oooh, baby, that beak is stuck gooooood!*" Dazz sang. "Talk to me, CP. Maybe the movement will loosen it up."

All Chicken Plant could do was groan.

Sleepy tugged at Chicken Plant's head. "We're making progress. Almost out. *Aaaaalmost* out. Just relax, and . . . ZZZZZZZZ." He collapsed on top of her, driving her beak even deeper into the ground.

"NOOOOO!" cried Hanazuki.

"*NOOOOO!*" sang Dazz.

"GROOOO!" groaned Chicken Plant.

Meanwhile, the Hemka barely noticed what was happening. Red was challenging Pink to steal one of Chicken Plant's feathers, but Pink was hugging Yellow, who could hardly breathe and was waving to Blue Hemka for help, who was sobbing to Green, who was having a tug-of-war with Lime Green over ear plugs they'd fashioned from Sleepy Unicorn's hair balls.

"MEE EER PLUU!" Green and Lime Green shouted over each other, until the hair balls partially unraveled, flew up into the air, and just so happened to land on Little Dreamer's back. He floated down in a onesie with OFF DUTY printed on the bum.

"Snoozy man! What great timing!" Hanazuki called to him, desperate to solve this fiasco, or at least part of this fiasco, and then take a much-deserved meditation break. "With your help, I can use a treasure to grow a tree that'll uproot Chicken Plant's beak! You in?"

Little Dreamer nodded but didn't drop a treasure.

"So about that treasure?" Hanazuki nudged.

"Shah la la," he whispered, shaking his OFF DUTY bum in Hanazuki's face. The loose hair balls dropped between Green and Lime Green, and they began tug-of-warring all over again.

"Really?! I'm all alone in this?" Hanazuki slumped down as the chaos seemed to build around her. What had gotten into her friends? Why couldn't they stay out of trouble? Was it boredom? Was it too much orange fruit juice? What could she do to get them to relax? To play nicely together? She put her head in her hands, while ideas to unite her moon whirled inside her brain. *Force everyone into moon-rock chairs and demand they chill!* No way. *Challenge them to play the "get along" game!* Nope. *Wait for pressing danger to motivate camaraderie!* Big. Fat. No.

Before Hanazuki could panic about what to do next, she felt an ear around her shoulder. She lifted her head and was met by Lavender Hemka, timid as ever. "Hey, little guy."

"See saw nee," he said softly.

Hanazuki tried to smile. "It's OK to say that. You're right. Our moon is going bananas for no good reason. You're always so inspiring, Lav— any ideas why?"

Lavender shrugged bashfully, then pointed at Yellow Hemka, who was jumping for joy . . . on Chicken Plant's stuck head. "Res lee cree eni."

"That's what you think?" Hanazuki asked. "That when bad stuff happens, our friends think of creative ways to save the day, but with no bad

stuff happening, all their creativity goes into making trouble?"

Lavender nodded, then covered his face with his ears.

"Aw, Lav. Don't get shy on me now—you're totally onto something! We need to help our friends put their creativity toward something positive. The question is how?"

Lavender opened his mouth to respond, but was interrupted by a series of rapid explosions in the sky. *Crack-pow! Crack-pow! Pow! Pow! Pow!*

What the—? Hanazuki hugged Lavender tight, and together, they ducked for cover while worries whipped around in her head. *What was happening? Was it the Big Bad? Was it more comets colliding in the sky? Was it something else, something worse?* By the time the explosions stopped, Hanazuki was brimming with a mix of curiosity and dread. She peeked up at the sky and . . . no Big Bad! No exploding comets! Instead, there was a superlong star-studded message.

LUNAVERSE'S GOT TALENT

A TALENT COMPETITION
ON CELEBRITY MOON
IN HALF A MOON CYCLE
GRAND PRIZE: A LIFELONG SUPPLY OF TREASURE TREES

THE DEETS

- EACH MOONFLOWER WILL DIRECT A TEAM OF THEIR ALTERLINGS AND/OR MOON CREATURES IN A PERFORMANCE.

- ONE TEAM PER MOON, WITH AN EXCEPTION FOR MOONFLOWERS WHO NO LONGER HAVE A MOON.

- ON CELEBRITY MOON, EACH TEAM WILL PEFORM FOR NO LONGER THAN FIVE MINUTES TO AN AUDIENCE OF CELEBRITY-MOON CREATURES. THE COMPETITION WILL ALSO BE BROADCAST ON THE BRAIN NETWORKS AND LATER ARCHIVED IN CELEBRITY MOON'S LIBRARY OF TALENT SHOWS.

- AFTER ALL TEAMS HAVE PERFORMED, A CELEBRITY JUDGE ALONGSIDE A COMMITTEE OF CELEBRITY-MOON CREATURES WILL DETERMINE THE WINNER.

Everybody was gawking at the message (including Chicken Plant, whose beak had apparently been freed by the explosion's vibrations). "Wow! Wow! Wow!" Hanazuki exclaimed, looking from the sky to her friends and then back at the sky. "Celebrity Moon—so weird. But cool. But weird!"

"Weird is right," Kiazuki said, suddenly hustling to Hanazuki's side. Kiyoshi shuffled in after her, his eyes peeled to the sky. Then, Maroshi surfed in with his favorite Flochi, Wanderer, perched on his shoulder. He gave the sky a double shaka sign.

"What do you think?" Hanazuki asked her Moonflower friends.

"I've got some questions," Kiyoshi said. "Or, like, a lot of questions."

"Then ask them," Kiazuki said. "Apparently there's a time cap on this whole thing."

Kiyoshi fired away. "Like, what is Celebrity Moon? Where is Celebrity Moon? Who is running this competition? Celebrity Moon's Moonflower? And why? What's in it for them?"

"Right on," Maroshi said. "Here's my Big Q. Will there really be a forever supply of Treasure Trees granted to the winner? Cause that would be mad life changing. I could finally build myself a home on a new, unexploded moon."

"And I could bring some color to my moon," added Kyoshi. "Black Treasure Trees are great and all, but my Little Unicorns deserve a vibrant place to zap each other."

Kiazuki waved her arms like *No way*. "It's impossible that any moon has such a surplus of trees that they can afford to give them away for life. Waaaaay too good to be true."

Hanazuki started to nod in agreement, but then Maroshi said, "Nah." He tossed up his spaceboard and spun it on his finger. "It's only too good to be true if you win."

"That's a cool trick," Hanazuki said, mesmerized.

"Oh, yeah?" Maroshi said. "Well, check it. If I were to compete in Lunaverse's Got Talent, I would do all kinds of rad surfer tricks with my Flochi—the snap, the tailslide, the alley-oop!"

"I don't know what you're saying," Kiazuki said flatly.

"I'll show you." Maroshi tossed his spaceboard in Rainbow Swirl Lake and hopped aboard, jumping and cutting and spinning on top of the Flochi-made waves. He exited the lake and shook out his blue hair. "How 'bout you, K-Man?" he asked Kiyoshi. "What have you got?"

"Me? Hmmm . . ." Kiyoshi scratched his head. "My Little Unicorns are pretty special."

"Yeah, they are," Maroshi said, snapping his fingers.

Kiyoshi smiled. "They can zap lightning bolts of power. Conduct message transmission. Transport Treasure Trees." His smile stretched. "I'm not sure what I can do, but their talents are AMAZING!"

"I can't believe you guys are actually

considering this," Kiazuki said. "Hanazuki, where you at? Please tell them this is dumb."

"Well . . ." Hanazuki bit her lip as she pictured putting together a super-cool act, traveling to a distant moon, and making forever memories. Hey, maybe she'd even get an endless supply of Treasure Trees out of it! "I dunno. I actually think it could be fun to do."

"What?! Are you kidding me?"

Just then, Little Dreamer floated down, wearing a onesie with ON DUTY printed on the bum. He dropped Hanazuki a treasure shaped like a trophy.

"Huzzah!" Hanazuki cried, jumping in the air. "This has to be a sign!" She faced Kiazuki. "So, yeah. Lunaverse's Got Talent? I'm totally in."

Before Kiazuki could scoff with jealousy, Little Dreamer dropped her a treasure shaped like a trophy, too. Hanazuki and Kiazuki looked at each other and broke into giggles. "I bet mine will pulse first," Kiazuki said.

"Nuh-uh, mine," Hanazuki said.

They stared at their treasures, hoping they'd blink a color—any color—even though they both knew that only a true mood moment could make that happen.

"How about this?" Hanazuki asked. "Whoever can grow a tree first through awesome inspiration and an awesome Lunaverse's Got Talent act wins!"

"Wins what?" Kiazuki asked.

"Wins . . . um . . ." Hanazuki thought about what she wanted. What she'd been craving for months. "A moon-spa day with absolutely NO distractions!" she blurted out. "I'm talking sunbathing by Rainbow Swirl Lake with a freshly squeezed glass of treasure-fruit juice."

"*Really?*"

"Yes, I'm being totally real. We can put a mini umbrella inside."

Kiazuki laughed. "Deal. You're on! You're so on!"

Maroshi ran a hand through his hair. "So I take it we're doing this?" he asked his fellow

Moonflowers. "Because if so, we should really get cracking."

"Always down for friendly competition," said Kiyoshi.

"That's the spirit!" said Hanazuki.

"You're all going D-O-W-N DOWN!" said Kiazuki.

They threw their hands into the middle of a huddle. "On three," Hanazuki said. "One, two—"

They exploded out of the huddle, shouting, "LUNAVERSE'S GOT TALENT!" Then, they scattered to prepare their acts.

Hanazuki was left alone with her Hemka and moon creature friends, who were back to causing more unnecessary trouble. Sleepy had conked out on top of Pink Hemka, who'd been dared by Purple Hemka to cross in front of Chicken Plant, whose beak was so crusted in moon dirt, she could barely open it.

What have I gotten myself into? Hanazuki wondered, her excitement withering into worry.

Do my friends really have the focus right now to put together an act? Can they even follow my directions? Her stomach churning, she waved Lavender over. He carefully hopped around Chicken Plant and then plopped into her lap. "What do you think about Lunaverse's Got Talent, little guy? Honestly, do we stand a chance at working as a team?"

Lavender looked up at the star-studded message. By now, it had lost most of its twinkle—the words were blurred and faded. But whatever twinkle was lost in the sky appeared in Lavender's eyes. "Zee perf chaz bing fenz too get! Ray za murl! Moo sha gen!!!"

Hanazuki grinned. "Huh. I mean, why not? This could be the perfect chance to bring our friends together."

As Lavender nodded, Hanazuki pictured Sleepy Unicorn and Dazzlessence and all of the Hemka combining their talents to make the COOLEST act of all time. "This *could* be amazing," she admitted, her heart rising in her chest. "Scratch that. It WILL be amazing!" She excitedly addressed the crowd.

"HELLO, MY AMAZINGLY TALENTED FRIENDS!" The moon creatures stopped what they were doing and looked at her expectantly. "We are going to put all of your unique creativity toward a collaboration that'll blow the celebrity judge and the Celebrity Moon creatures' minds! Who's with me?"

The moon creatures shot their arms up with an enthusiastic, "WOO!"

"Everybody take the next hour to come up with ideas, and then we'll come together at the crater by the Safety Cave to see what we've got. I'm so excited to direct all of you!"

As some of the moon creatures applauded and others eagerly dispersed to plan, Hanazuki put her hand out for a shake. Lavender shook back.

"You and me, Lav—let's get this competition started. Celebrity Moon—ready or not, here we come!!!"

CHAPTER TWO

CASTING CALL

"O K, OK, so let's go over our list again," Hanazuki said to Lavender as they sat in Talking Pyramid's shade, shaking with a mix of excitement and nerves. It was hard to believe forty-five minutes had passed since the announcement had appeared in the sky. Time sure did fly when you were planning a show!

Lavender held up the notepad.

"'Lunaverse's Got Talent Prep,'" read Hanazuki. "'First, hear everybody's ideas and decide what kind of amazing act to do. Second, make sure our friends are having the time of their lives and working well together. Third, try to win.'" She looked at Lavender. "It's a short list, but also *a lot* to think about. Like, where do we begin?"

"Wuz zee ba za," Lavender assured her.

"You're right," Hanazuki said, waving her worries away. "I'll take it one step at a time. There's only so much I can do before everyone pitches their ideas. I hope the role of director suits me. You think it suits me?"

Lavender nodded, then pretended to slate with his ears.

Hanazuki joined in on the joke. "And . . . action!" she said, then peered out in front of her, like the whole moon was her stage. Except down on the moon ground, her view was kind of obstructed. "Hey, TP! Whaddya see up there?"

"Well," Talking Pyramid said, then stopped.

"What is it?" Hanazuki asked.

Talking Pyramid sighed, then let it all fall out of his mouth. "Maroshi's surfing in Rainbow Swirl Lake, training Wanderer to spit water high in the sky, like a fountain. Kiazuki's in a Treasure Tree

garden, working on choreography to the beat of Zikoro's barking. Kiyoshi's training his Little Unicorns to leap through rings. Well, trying to train them. They are mostly zapping one another, occasionally missing, and setting the rings on fire." He paused. "You two are clinging to me rather tightly."

"Ha! We're not clinging," Hanazuki said defensively, stepping out from Talking Pyramid's shadow. "We're chillaxing while learning all about our competition."

"So it's *not* that you're panicking now that you know the other Moonflowers are rehearsing their incredibly impressive acts?"

"Ugh, fine. Yes," Hanazuki replied, shrugging and nodding her head. "Moonsocks, you're good."

"That's what creatures tell me. Look, I believe in you and your friends, Hana Z. But life isn't about sitting in shade, sort-of-not-really planning for great things to happen. It's about making great things happen."

"Roger that." Hanazuki quickly but gently peeled Lavender's ears off Talking Pyramid. "We've got to get to our friends!" she told him. "The clock is ticking!"

She and Lavender raced toward the closest Mouth Portal but were still a ways away when Little Dreamer swooped down with a burnt ring around his middle left over from Kiyoshi's rehearsal. "Hey, snoozy dude!" Hanazuki said, panting. "Think we can get a ride?"

"Shee la za," Little Dreamer whispered, dipping toward the ground.

"I'm gonna take that as a yes." Lavender jumped on Hanazuki's back as Hanazuki gripped the Hula-Hoop. In a blink, Little Dreamer was whisking them up into the air.

"Wooooooo-eeeeeeee!" Hanazuki and Lavender cried together, the crisp wind whipping at their cheeks. They jetted over the other Moonflowers, flew low to the crater by the Safety Cave, and jumped from Little Dreamer's back.

Hanazuki and Lavender spotted their friends, strangely standing in a line. Had she told them to meet in a line? At the front, acting like the creature in charge, was Dazzlessence Jones. Hanazuki jogged over to him. "Hey, Dazz! Did you get everyone lined up?"

"Hanazuki!" he exclaimed. "Yes, yes, I did. H, this is our *audition line*. As producer—"

"Producer?"

"You're welcome for stepping in," Dazz said. "As *producer*, it's important to me that we stay organized."

"Oh! That's cool! I just kind of imagined us sitting in a circle and discussing our ideas—"

"*Discussing,* ha! How civil of you. How naïve. *Auditions* are an essential part of any show, and to cast the *best* show, we've got to be cutthroat."

"'Cutthroat'?" Hanazuki repeated, suddenly itching with worry.

"*Excuse me,*" Dazzlessence sang, then strolled down the line. "Ladies and gentle-creatures, if you haven't checked in with me, please raise your hand."

Everyone raised their hands. Except Basal Ganglia, who was a literal brain. He just raised an eyebrow.

"*OK, coming to meet and greet ya!*" Dazz sang. "Remember—*you shine, I shine. I shine when you shine! In line or onstage, Lunaverse's Got Talent is where it's at!*"

Hanazuki swallowed, a lump forming in the back of her throat. It was awesome to see all of her friends ready to be a part of the act, and she guessed it was fine that Dazzlessence was taking on a producer role. But would Dazz put all his focus on *winning* and neglect the *fun, collaborative* part of the process? How could her friends be freely creative under his pressure?

Hanazuki watched Purple and Pink take a break from warming up their voices, and she leaped at the opportunity to direct. "Hey, great work!" she said, greeting them. "Pink, why don't you try singing a step higher? The harmony'll sound incredible that way!"

Pink wailed a high note, and it clashed with Purple's tenor.

"*Dissonance much?*" Dazzlessence scoffed in passing, stopping Pink and Purple in their vocal tracks.

Hanazuki winced. "Don't worry, little guys. It didn't gel that time, but if you keep practicing—"

"Yay a yee yeee?" Purple cut in.

"Oh, no, I'm not auditioning," Hanazuki replied with a smile. "With so much talent here and the chance to bring it all together, I'm really excited to direct."

They looked at her like she had two Moodblossoms.

"Anyway, just keep doin' your thang!" Hanazuki pranced off before they could see her cheeks turn beet red. *Maybe I can help Green before Dazz gets to him first*, she told herself, approaching him mid ear stretch. "Nice, Green," she encouraged. "Breathe through it, my man!" But Green had new hairy earplugs in, and so he didn't hear her. That, or he was choosing not to listen, stretching no deeper than he was before.

"*You call that a stretch?*" Dazz sang, clapping in Green's face. Feeling insecure, Green bent his body over his ear hard and fast, then yelped in pain.

"Oh, Green! Do you need ice?" Hanazuki asked.

Green took an earplug out. "Ja?"

"I was asking if you need ice. But also, you should breathe and stretch however you like—this is *your* audition, OK?"

Green blinked blankly, then reblocked his ear.

"So no ice, got it," Hanazuki mumbled, feeling totally useless. She looked down at Lavender, trailing in her shadow. "Is it just me or is Dazz souring everyone's attitudes?"

Lavender shrugged, then nodded. "Gah?"

"I feel ya. I'm confused, too. I'm glad my friends are motivated to do Lunaverse's Got Talent—that's great!—but I just wish they would let me support them."

Hanazuki stared at Lavender, waiting for his brilliant inspiration. But as the seconds ticked by, the pressure seemed to paralyze him. "Sorry, didn't mean to put you on the spot," she said, then caught sight of Dazz over Lavender's shoulder, collecting Lime Green's headshot. "Keep thinking, not freaking. I'll be right back."

She hustled to Dazz's side as he was collecting Purple's headshot. "Hey there, my shiny friend."

"Hi, my less-shiny friend," Dazz said. "No offense. It's just that I'm a diamond."

"Right. None taken. Anyway," she plowed on, "it's great that you're stepping into the role of producer, but now that I'm here and ready to jump into gear, you can leave the direction to me!"

"*Sure thing*," Dazz sang, shuffling the headshots into one clean stack and handing them over to her. "Why don't you take a seat, H. We're about to get started with the auditions."

Well, that was easy, Hanazuki thought. "Thanks, Dazz! I knew you'd understand!" She strolled to the black folding chair in front of the stage. About to sit, Dazz swooped in before her bum could make a landing.

"This is the producer's chair," he told her.

"Oh," Hanazuki said, looking around for the director's chair. There was no such thing, so, a little embarrassed, she sat cross-legged on the ground. As she watched the moon creatures finish rolling up their spines, singing their last vocal ladders, and taking their final looks in their handheld mirrors, she wondered how she could be more helpful. "Dazz, what exactly does a producer do?"

"Everything I'm already doing."

"But then, what do *I* do?"

"Direct."

"But you seem to be directing."

"I oversee the direction."

"Do I oversee the production?"

"Of course. You're the Moonflower."

"Exactly!" Hanazuki gave a sigh of relief. "That's great to hear, because I was starting to think—"

Dazz glanced at the sign-up sheet. "First up," he announced, cutting her off. "Blue Hemka."

Hanazuki itched to say, "Wait, so *am* I being heard?" but Blue Hemka was already climbing onto the stage, gripping an onion, and launching into his audition. He went *chop, chop, chop* with his ears and tried not to cry. His eyes turned glassy, then welled up right as he finished his last chop. He quickly hopped offstage with his head held high . . . to keep the waterworks from spilling down his cheeks. It worked! He resisted the tears!

"You're not crying, but I'M crying!" Hanazuki called, applauding. "Can we see it again, this time with—"

"NEXT!" Dazz called, cutting her off again.

"Just a sec," Hanazuki said, jumping to her feet. "As *director*, I would like to give Blue some positive feedback and direction."

Dazz stared at her like, *Really? Now?* He motioned to Blue in the audience, who was proudly flicking away the tears racing down his cheeks. Then, he motioned to Orange Hemka and Green Hemka onstage, who were earnestly waiting for their cue.

"Well, I don't want to stop the flow," Hanazuki said, "but—"

"*Perfect!*" Dazz sang. "Moving on!"

Hanazuki felt an anxious ball in the pit of her stomach as she dropped down to her bum. *Relax*, she told herself. *Enjoy the auditions and you can boost your friends up and give them direction later.* Luckily, as she watched wacky audition after wacky audition, the ball of anxiety seemed to unravel itself.

Audition 2: Orange Hemka tucked a floppy ear inside his eardrum, balanced a treasure fruit on it, and then let his ear flop out, propelling the fruit into Green Hemka's mouth. Green Hemka bit the fruit, and its juice sprayed all over a flat slab of moon rock like experimental art.

Audition 3: Red Hemka closed his mouth and blew steam out his ears.

Audition 4: Lime Green Hemka conducted a palm/ear reading on Dazzlessence Jones. Instead of telling Dazz's future, he shrieked, freaking everyone out. Especially Dazz.

Audition 5: Purple Hemka and Pink Hemka

sang a love song together, in harmony, using "*ya ya yoo*" sounds only.

Audition 6: Teal Hemka and Yellow Hemka fashioned chic Moonflower bow ties.

Audition 7: Doughy Bunington built a cupcake castle.

Audition 8: Basal Ganglia did stand-up comedy. He started, "So a brain walks into a bar . . ."

Audition 9: Sleepy Unicorn performed a Moonspeare monologue, but got so sleepy so fast, that he ad-libbed and then passed out. "To be or definitely not to be? I have a question. I can't remember the question. The question is . . . ZZZZZZZ."

After some laughter, there was a pause. Dazzlessence was scribbling on the audition forms. Hanazuki glanced at them. Was he taking that many notes? Should she have been taking notes? She took a closer look to see if they had any overlapping ideas, but there were no ideas. The page was filled with Dazz's own signature.

"Dazz? Your autograph looks great, but do you think you can check to see if we have any final performers?"

But somehow Dazz had disappeared from his chair.

Hanazuki's attention snapped back to the stage, where she heard a timid voice ask, "Ya yoo froo?" Lavender was standing center stage, still as a moon rock. Except for his ears. They were twitching.

"Oh, hey, Lav!" she gushed. "I'm so glad you're auditioning, too!"

"Ya," he croaked.

"So what have you got for us today?"

"Nu va."

"It's normal to feel nervous when you're alone onstage. But don't worry. We're all here to support you. Be brave and do your best. I believe in you!"

After a few moments, Lavender began droning, "Luuuuuuu," which was like "Uhhhhhh" in Hemka-speak.

"Are you ready?" she gently pressed.

"Na na?" he asked.

"Yup! Now's good!"

Lavender took a deep breath. He swayed back and forth, gathering momentum. Hanazuki could hardly contain herself. She was so proud to see her timid buddy break out of his shell! He hopped forward, then backward, then forward, *faster*, *faster*, *faster*, gaining speed until—

"*DAZZ and his JAZZ are HEEEEEEEEEEEEERE!*"

In a blinding fury, Dazzlessence raced onto the stage in glitter wristbands, a matching glitter dance belt, and taps on the soles of his cowboy boots. "Hit it," he demanded, pointing past the audience to Orange Hemka, who was now inside the sound booth. Orange pressed a button, setting off country music with a hard beat. Dazz began pirouetting—one, two, three, forty-six in a row. With every turn, his sparkle sparkled sparklier.

Hanazuki's body vibrated with the music. Before she knew it, her feet were tapping and her hands were clapping and her vocal cords were ripping, "WOOOOOO!" She wasn't alone—the whole crowd was going nuts!

Dazzlessence performed his final move—a leap into a split! It was then, in a moment of stillness, that Hanazuki noticed Lavender Hemka huddled in the upstage corner. Her heart sank. Lavender had almost put on a brave face. He'd almost auditioned in front of all their friends. He'd almost broken out of his shell.

Instead, Dazz had stolen his thunder.

Hanazuki needed to make this right. Maybe if she cheered Lavender's name, he'd give his audition another go! She started chanting, slowly, hoping it would catch on. "*Lav-en-der! Lav-en-der! Lav-en-der!*" But no one caught on. Probably because no one could hear her over the much louder chanting, "*Ja-zzy Dazz! Ja-zzy Dazz! Ja-zzy Dazz!*"

Orange Hemka began blasting exit music, while Red Hemka tossed roses onto the stage. "*Keep 'em coming,*" Dazz sang. "If you want to be cast, throw roses. *All of you!* Throw roses at my beautiful, tappy feet!"

Hanazuki ran to Orange, raised her hand to her neck, and gave him the "cut it" gesture. He cut it. "Hey, Dazz?" she called to the stage.

"Yes, a question from the audience," Dazz said, motioning to Hanazuki.

"We've got one more performer."

"Do we?"

"It's Lavender. Can we give him another shot?"

Lavender shrank into himself. She guessed Dazz's number was a hard one to follow. Especially for the timidest little guy on the moon.

Hanazuki pushed on, "I think maybe with some encouragement—"

"It's for the best," Dazz broke in. AGAIN. "It's always good to end on the *strongest noooooote!*" He sang a high C and then riffed down to a low C. "Don't worry, L-buddy. There's always next year. Maybe. We'll see." He scanned the audience. "Next question!"

Before Hanazuki could protest, Dazz had called on Sleepy Unicorn. "When does the cast list go up?" he asked.

"Thanks for asking about my child-star past," Dazz replied.

"I, uh, didn't," Sleepy said.

Dazz plowed on. "As a toddler, I didn't toddle. My first steps were a jazz square. After that, I took all sorts of dance classes, studying under the major studs of the stage. I performed with them for audiences of opals and garnets and rubies and jades. I won so many competitions, I became known as 'Jazzy Dazz.' Which is why it's dazzling to hear that nickname chanted for me now!"

"You told us we had to call you Jazzy Dazz," said Sleepy.

"*We've got a comedian in the houuuuuuse!*" Dazz sang. He stood firm, suddenly serious. "Sleepy, you're out. Red, you're a goner. Green, buh-bye. Lavender, not a chance."

"Whaaa? Hold up, Dazz," Hanazuki interjected. "The whole point of participating in Lunaverse's Got Talent is to bring everybody together!"

Dazz shook his head. "Winning the grand prize will bring everybody together. Beating out the other Moonflowers will, too. We can't compete with Kiyoshi's Little Unicorns or Maroshi's Flochi or Kiazuki's Zikoro." He paused. "Well, we might beat Kiazuki's Zikoro. But we won't beat out any other Moonflower's team of alterlings if we don't put together an *amaaaaaaazing* show! Sure, everybody brought their talents to the table, but *some talents* are *shinier* than *others*." He pointed to himself. "If you get what I mean."

Hanazuki sighed. *Was Dazz right?* Maybe with a show made up of the "cream of the crop," they'd have a better chance at winning. And if they won, her moon could come together in celebration. The lump in the back of her throat seemed to grow. She glanced at her friends. What did they want more: to be in the show or to win?

"*Earth to Hanazuki*," Dazz sang, waving a hand in front of her face.

"Huh?" Hanazuki wiped the sweat from her forehead. She'd wanted so badly to be a good leader for her team, but being in the spotlight felt like being in a pressure cooker. "I think . . ." The ball of anxiety was back in the pit of her stomach. She didn't know what she thought. She didn't know what was best.

"We win this thing, and the glory is everybody's to share," nudged Dazz.

"Ya! Ya! Ya!" Orange Hemka, Yellow Hemka, and Blue Hemka cried in agreement.

"To be the best act or not to be the best act, that is the question," inserted Sleepy.

"Cut the non-cream of the crop and let's move on," jeered Basal Ganglia.

"I guess," Hanazuki surrendered, crossing her fingers that they were right. "This is a team effort. So if this is what you, as a team, think is best, let's give it a shot."

CHAPTER THREE

ACTING OUT

*T*hree *days till the show, ooooh baby*," Dazzlessence sang to the cast and crew. "Crunch time. Focus time. Make-me-shine time!"

Hanazuki did everything in her power not to cringe. These last several days, she hadn't been directing so much as trying to keep Dazz in check and the cast and crew motivated. Everybody had auditioned to be in the show, but only five moon creatures had made the final cut. The designers felt like they had no creative license. The backup dancers felt underused. Sleepy couldn't stop falling asleep, and as Hanazuki's team had grown more and more resentful, they'd begun to act out. Worse than before!

Hanazuki studied the cast list, wishing she could collect the courage to finally take charge, to stand up for her friends, to show them that their talents were wonderful no matter what Dazz told them!

SHINING STAR AND PRODUCER—DAZZLESSENCE JONES

DIRECTOR—HANAZUKI

BACKUP DANCERS—ORANGE HEMKA, YELLOW HEMKA, BLUE HEMKA, PURPLE HEMKA

CHOREOGRAPHER—SLEEPY UNICORN

PROPS MASTER—DOUGHY BUNINGTON

SOUND ENGINEER—LIME GREEN HEMKA

LIGHTING DESIGNER—GREEN HEMKA

THE SPOTLIGHT—PINK HEMKA

CROWD ENERGIZER—RED HEMKA

COSTUME DESIGNER—TEAL HEMKA

STAGE MANAGER—LAVENDER HEMKA

Feeling as uninspired as a dried-up Rainbow

Swirl Lake, Hanazuki dropped the list and brought her focus to the stage, where Sleepy was teaching the cast the latest choreography. "*Shake, shake, shake*," he instructed, shaking his bum. "Greatest move in show business. Frees up your whole body."

Dazz put a hand on his hip. "Lime Green, the music please."

Lime Green pressed play. The music was so faint, Hanazuki could hardly make out the beat.

"Louder," Dazz demanded.

Lime Green turned down the music.

"No, up." The music went practically silent. "Hello? Stage manager—you back there? Lavender peeked his head out. "Can you do something about this?"

"Ya yee zug strah," Lavender explained.

"Loud music stresses Lime Green out," Hanazuki translated.

"Then *why* is he running *sound?!*" Dazz exclaimed.

Sleepy threw off his jazz shoes and, without realizing it, nailed Dazzlessence in the stomach. "Ah, much better," he drawled. "I don't like shoes."

Dazz groaned, then chucked Sleepy's jazz shoes into the wings. "Are we doing this, *choreographer*?"

"I love when you call me that," Sleepy said. "Has a nice ring." He looked at the performers. "I would like to cast a dance solo from the ensemble. Yellow, come front and center."

Hanazuki clapped for Yellow. His joy was contagious—what a great choice! Yellow started hopping downstage, but Purple beat him to the spotlight. "No, Purple," Hanazuki said. "It's Yellow's turn."

Orange pushed Purple out of the way, who knocked into Blue.

"No, Orange," Hanazuki said. "Like I just said, it's Yellow's turn."

Blue started to cry.

"*Forget them*," Dazz sang, sliding into the

spotlight. "I'll be front and center the whole time." He faced Sleepy. "We've been bum-shaking for an hour. We get it. Time to move on to the moonwalk!"

"Great idea," Sleepy said. "Dancers, now moonwalk." He demonstrated by jumping up and down.

Hanazuki didn't know what made moonwalking different from normal walking, but she was pretty sure it was different from jumping. Dazz had his face in his hands, which confirmed her suspicions. "Dazz, want to tell us what a moonwalk is?" she urged.

"Forget telling, dum-dums. *I'll show you.*" Dazzlessence glided backward across the stage while appearing to walk forward. Then he stopped, waiting for Red, the crowd energizer, to initiate uproarious applause.

Instead, a wagon rolled onto the stage. Inside was Basal Ganglia, cracking a joke. "So a brain walks into a bar—"

"You were cut from the show, Basal," Dazz snapped. "*C-U-T*! *Cut*! Do you know what that means?"

"Scissors."

"Huh?" Dazz pointed at Basal and stomped his feet. "Lavender, how did Basal get on stage?"

"Like I was saying," Basal said, "a brain walks into a bar and asks, 'Do you have any potato chip–flavored helicopters?' The waiter replies, 'No, we only have plane.'"

Crickets. Except for Orange, who burst into hysterical laughter.

Lavender began to wheel Basal offstage. "I'm the BRAINS! I'm the STAR! I'm driving a FANCY CAR!" he shouted. "*Beep beep!*" He pushed out his lobes and pretended to steer the wagon.

With Basal finally back in the wings, Hanazuki hoped that they could carry on with rehearsal, but then Pink, acting as the spotlight, began hopping around the stage. The cast began chasing him. Yellow pushed Purple, who shoved Orange, who tickled Dazz, who exploded into a spin that knocked everybody in a five-foot radius to their bums.

This was getting ridiculous. "Hey, Pink, can you hop offstage?" Hanazuki called to him. But his hopping continued. Plus, he began to shriek. "Green?" she called to the lighting booth. "Green, can you cut the spotlight? Get Pink to stop?" More lights kicked in. "GREEN, WHAT ARE YOU DOING?!"

"Jah?" he finally replied, cool as a cucumber.

"The lights," Hanazuki said.

He dimmed them. "Cha chull."

"Yeah, real chill. But we're not looking for mood lighting. This isn't a café—this is a performance."

Green turned all the lights on at once, cueing Teal Hemka to wheel in a wardrobe. Teal dressed Dazz in a white jumpsuit.

"*I can't move in this,*" Dazz sang in discomfort. "It's like being in a straitjacket."

Teal dashed offstage, giggling.

"That's because it *is* a straitjacket," Hanazuki moaned. "Hey Lavender, can you bring out the actual costumes? The ones the cast are *supposed* to dance in."

Lavender wheeled Basal Ganglia back onstage. He was wearing a dozen sequined neckties. "The costumes chose ME," he said. "Who's the STAR CZAR now? MWAH HA HA HA HEE HEE—" He broke into a cough. "Ow! These neckties are choking me. Subjects, free my lobes! I demand a clip-on!"

Yellow and Orange removed the ties from Basal Ganglia, while Hanazuki helped Dazz out of the jumpsuit.

"I find this very unfair," Doughy Bunington piped up from the wings. "I'm just sitting here, eating my feelings, and no one has come over to ask if I want to be the lead of the show."

"You want to be the lead of the show?" Hanazuki asked flatly.

"Obviously. *Cupcakes by Doughy* are all the

rage, and the more face time I get on Celebrity Moon, the better they'll sell. Maybe I'll even get a celebrity endorsement."

Dazz knocked the top cupcake off Doughy's cupcake castle. The icing splattered onto the stage floor. "You know what's all the *rage*?"

"Mini cupcakes in the shape of a boat?"

"*MEEEE!* Three days from now, I'll be the biggest celebrity in the galaxy. You'll be crawling on your hands and lower bun to get me to shoot a cupcake commercial." He addressed the whole team. "Listen up! If you feel like your talents are being underused, and if that bruises your pudgy little egos, then *put a bandage on it!*"

"Band-Aids don't work on brains," Basal said. "It's like tape on wax."

"Why are you STILL HERE?"

"Dazz," Hanazuki jumped in, "Maybe take a breather, a long walk—"

"No time for *BREATHING* or *WALKING* or anything with the word '*LONG*'! Sleepy, *KEEP*

CHOREOGRAPHING." But Sleepy was at the foot of the stage, sprawled out and snoring.

Oh boy, Hanazuki thought. She scrambled to nudge him awake, when his dream appeared through a holographic projection. It was a really old childhood memory . . .

Kid Sleepy Unicorn was working backstage at a talent show. Tensions were high between Kid

Dazzlessence and his disgruntled cousin, Kid Randy—a cubic zirconia. In a fit of jealousy over Kid Dazz's natural talent and real shine, Kid Randy tried to make Kid Dazz's act fail. He coated the stage with goo. He sewed up Kid Dazz's costume too tight. He messed with the music.

But every attempted sabotage worked in Kid Dazz's favor. Kid Dazz slid onto the stage like a rock star. He burst out of his costume like a ripped warrior. He improvised to the new music, dancing more dazzlingly than he had with his original choreography.

After the act, Kid Randy told Kid Dazz, "Listen up, cuz! The next time you compete in a talent competition, it will destroy you. You hear me?"

"I hear you," Kid Dazz said, "but—"

"DESTROY YOUUUUUU!" Kid Randy screamed.

Kid Sleepy tried to mediate. "You two are family!" he said. "Sure, one of you is a real diamond and the other is a fake diamond sold on the market at a far more affordable price, but you're both sparkly talents!"

But it was too late. "Destruction," mouthed Kid Randy before knocking Kid Dazz to the floor. "Just you wait."

As Hanazuki gasped, Sleepy jerked awake and the projection dissolved. "Shall we pop-and-lock?" he asked the cast. No one responded. "Y'all sure are quiet. Are we good to go, my interplanetary dancers?"

"Um," Hanazuki replied, her heart slamming in her chest. "Keep choreographing while I chat with Dazz."

"No need to be wary of it," Sleepy said mid-yawn. "Pop-and-lock is a winning move."

"Uh-huh." Hanazuki dragged Dazz into the wings and pushed him into his producer's chair. "What do you think?"

"I like the pop-and-lock all right."

"No, about Sleepy's dream! About you and Randy!"

"Oh, that guy?" Dazz waved his hand, all carefree. "Cause Randy is *harmless*. He's a synthetic jewel who's never followed through with *anything in his life*. He doesn't have the work ethic to pull off whatever he was *threatening to pull off*."

"A curse."

"*Riiiight*," Dazz sang, pretending to shake in his boots. "A curse!"

Hanazuki started to chew her fingernails. She didn't know much about cousin rivalry, but she did know enough about sibling rivalry from Sleepy Unicorn and Twisted Unicorn to know that the threat of destruction was no laughing matter. "I think you should give up your role," she said, pacing up and down the length of the wings. "To keep your participation under wraps."

"Say what?! *Are you out of your moon mind, H?* Me? Not perform?"

"Just in case Randy's threat is real!"

Dazz put a hand on Hanazuki's shoulder. "I promise you that Randy has the stamina of a sloth with congestion. The fake diamond can barely perform, let alone pose any threat to Lunaverse's Got Talent."

"Maybe. It's just—"

"*Definitely.* That talent show was a long, *looooong* time ago! We were just kids! As producer, I am not going to ruin our act because of some jealous episode on the ancient past. Unless you want a maniac brain to take the lead?"

Basal bowed. "I'm here, Hanazuki, and gladly accept the starring role."

"*MY MOON GOD, YOU WERE CUT!!!*" Dazz sang, then hurried back onstage, where Sleepy Unicorn had begun demonstrating the bend-and-snap. "Dancy 'Corn, take five!"

"Five minutes or—?"

"*Minutes, hours, years, whateeeeevs.* I'm choreographing now." Dazz pointed to the stage. "All right, moonstuds, show me what you've got.

And a one, kick, two, sashay. Chins up! Toes pointed!" While the cast tried to follow the dance calls and the design team tried to spontaneously adjust the lights and sound, Dazz barged into the spotlight. "Adios, Yellow," he said, shoving him out of the way. "I'm producing, choreographing, and starring in this act!"

Hanazuki stood there, stunned. How had things gotten so out of hand? How had she let *Dazz* get so out of hand?

Just then, Little Dreamer swooped down from the sky to the back of the audience. He seemed to be staying as far away from the chaos as possible. Hanazuki didn't blame him. But, catching a glimpse of Lavender with his head in his ears, she started to blame herself.

Hanazuki took a deep breath, and then, before she could overthink it, she mounted the stage. "LISTEN UP, EVERYONE!" she called. "AND I MEAN EVERYONE, *DAZZ*." The music stopped. Pink shape-shifted out of a spotlight. The house lights flicked on. "We are all friends. We are a team. If we can't act that way, we shouldn't do the competition at all."

Unhappy murmurs erupted from the stage.

"*What are you even taaaaalking about?*" Dazz sang.

"You mean quit?" Doughy Bunington asked, flabbergasted.

Blue began to bawl. Orange yelped in defiance. Yellow yipped in shock. Purple began stomping. Lime Green started to shriek. Red finally tried to energize the crowd with a "BA! BA! BA!" call-and-response, but the audience was empty—everybody was either onstage or in the wings.

"Hey, I don't want to quit any more than you do," Hanazuki said. "But if we do this, something's gotta give."

Little Dreamer plopped down beside her. "Wazzee woo," he whispered, getting so close, it was as if he was telling her to climb aboard again.

Hanazuki grabbed onto his onesie. Sure enough,

Little Dreamer floated up like a balloon, lifting her into the sky. "WE'VE GOT THREE DAYS LEFT!" she shouted to the crowd below, her voice piercing through the atmosphere. "THAT'S NOT ENOUGH TIME TO CHANGE THE ACT, BUT IT IS ENOUGH TIME TO COMMIT. LUNAVERSE'S GOT TALENT IS BIGGER THAN YOU. BIGGER THAN ME. BIGGER THAN ANY OF US. AND IF WE'RE GOING TO BLOW CELEBRITY MOON AWAY, LIKE DAZZ SAYS WE ARE, WE'RE GOING TO NEED TO SET ASIDE OUR DIFFERENCES AND *COMMIT, COOPERATE, AND COME TOGETHER*!!!"

Little Dreamer spun in circles, and Hanazuki's skirt twirled out like an umbrella. "CHANT IT WITH ME: *TOGETHER WE SOAR! TOGETHER WE SOAR!*" Her friends—cast, crew, designers alike—chanted, "*Together we soar! Together we soar!*" Then with growing voices and enthusiasm, "*TOGETHER WE SOAR! TOGETHER WE SOAR!*" The chanting grew even stronger as Hanazuki was lowered to the ground. Lavender raced to her for a hug, and as they embraced, Hanazuki's Moodblossom began pulsing lavender.

"I'm all for commitment," Dazz sang, suddenly waving Hanazuki to a private, upstage nook. "But with three days left? What do you think can happen? How much of the act can we realistically *change*?"

He had a point. "You started this journey," Hanazuki said, "but we're here to finish it, together." She put a hand on his shoulder. "Pursue your vision, Dazz, but let us help you. Let's support one another as best we can, and then maybe, *just maybe*, we can bring home those Treasure Trees. You in?"

Dazz took a moment to think as his face flashed from embarrassment to regret to guilt. Then he spun wildly, ready for a fresh-tastic start. "Let's do this."

CHAPTER FOUR

A ROCKY ROAD

"It's the day of the show, y'all!" Hanazuki cheered as her cast and crew added the finishing touches to their hair and makeup and set design, gushing with excitement. "Let's run it one last time before we depart!"

"Plah-sa!" Lavender called out.

"Places!" Hanazuki translated. As the cast scrambled to their opening spots, she sat in front of the stage to watch their final run-through before takeoff.

Dazz tapped his cowboy boots together. "*And a one, a two, a one, two, threeee!*"

The beat kicked in. Lavender pulled up the curtain. Green shone light onto the edge of the stage. Sleepy Unicorn threw back two orange-fruit juice tablets, which apparently had mega caffeine-like energy, then swaggered on, rapping, *"To be or not to be? That is the question."*

"Keep it up, Sleepy!" Hanazuki called, glad she'd chosen him to introduce the number. "Eyes wide with sleepless pride!"

The spotlight hopped off. Colorful strobe lights kicked in. The ensemble burst onstage. Dazz slid center and break-danced. Then he spun. Then he shuffled. Then he did the limbo. Meanwhile, the Hemka grabbed cupcakes from Doughy Bunington's cupcake castle and constructed an edible boat. Sleepy Unicorn hopped inside and everybody pretended to row it offstage. Just when the act seemed to be over, the cast exploded back onstage for a tap-dance extravaganza at double speed!

The music cut out. All Hanazuki could hear were the panting performers and the rapid beating of her own heart. Lavender snuck out from backstage, and Hanazuki gave him a double thumbs-up. She wished she had ten more thumbs. A million more thumbs. "We've got an act like no other," she beamed. "A *winning* act like no other!!!"

The cast and crew went wild, waving their sequined belts in the air like lassos. Little Dreamer, with cucumbers over his eyes, flipped in the air.

The wager! Hanazuki suddenly remembered, feeling a rush of inspiration. She peeked at her trophy treasure. It was blinking. So were her bracelet and plume. Booyah! Her act was going to be a sensation! The Celebrity Moon creatures were going to jump to their feet in a standing O! The celebrity judge was going to be blown away. "I'm blown away," they would say. "I grant you and your moon a forever supply of Treasure Trees."

"Forever?" Hanazuki would ask politely, just to confirm.

"Forever-evah," the celebrity judge would confirm.

Then, Treasure Trees would rain from the sky and land on top of Hanazuki's spacesurfer. She'd zip back and forth between moons, carrying a few at a time, and plant them in the shape of a giant microphone!

"Time to go," Kiazuki said, startling Hanazuki from her daydream.

"Did you see my team's act?" she blurted out.

"I did not," Kiazuki replied.

"Well, if you had seen 'em," said Hanazuki, "your jaw would be on the floor."

"Well, if you'd seen Zikoro and me," said Kiazuki, "your jaw would be thirty feet under the moon dust."

Just then, Maroshi surfed up on his spaceboard. "Today is the day!" he cried. "Can't wait to do my sick tricks! You have no idea how totally surf-tastic my Flochi are."

"Well, you have no idea how space-tastic my Hemka and friends are," said Hanazuki.

"Well, you have no idea how hip-hop-tastic Zikoro is," said Kiazuki.

They stared one another down, then broke into giggles.

"On that note," Hanazuki said, "Lunaverse's Got Talent is a far ways away—we gotta go!"

Maroshi gave Hanazuki and Kiazuki a shaka sign. "See ya on the other side."

Kiazuki and Zikoro boarded their spacesurfer, and Maroshi and his Flochi boarded their spaceboard.

"Bon voyage," Maroshi called, surfing ahead.

Hanazuki and her team boarded their spacesurfer, too. Doughy Bunington had opted to stay behind—spacesurfer treats were the worst! Green and Red were "feeling under the weather," though as they'd told Hanazuki on the down low, they were really staying back to plan a surprise cast party for when everybody returned from Celebrity Moon. Basal Ganglia was intentionally left in the Safety Cave—for everybody else's safety.

"We're comin' for you, Celebrity Moon!" Hanazuki cried. Packed in like space sardines, she flew her friends off into the atmosphere. Almost immediately, Dazzlessence Jones began leading them in a series of vocal warm-ups.

"Red leather, yellow leather," said Dazz.

"Red leather, yellow leather," repeated the cast.

"Space boat, space boat, space boat," said Dazz.

"Space boat, space boat, space boat," repeated the cast.

"Gal in the galaxy, galaxy gal," said Dazz.

"Gal in the galaxy, galaxy gal," repeated the cast.

Halfway there, Hanazuki felt a rush of nerves. After all her team had had to overcome in the last three days, the pressure to win was on. Her friends must have felt the pressure, too. Dazzlessence was obsessively shining his body, and Sleepy Unicorn was mumbling his rap lyrics on repeat. Though most of the Hemka seemed too excited for nerves. Traveling to a new moon—Celebrity Moon at that—was going to be something they'd remember forever!

As soon as Hanazuki's nerves settled down, a wave of turbulence hit. With it came gusts of wind. Zooming meteors. Colicky comets. The spacesurfer vibrated, rocked, twisted, and dropped. Everyone began screaming. Hanazuki's heart began pounding out of her chest. She tried her best to steer clear of the galaxy's debris, but the racket her friends were making wasn't helping. She signaled Dazz to distract them.

"*Dazzy dared me to dash my denim ends!*" sang Dazz.

"*Dazzy dared me—AHHHHHH!*" sang the cast.

"*Big Dipper dips deeper 'n' Little Dipper leaps lower!*" sang Dazz.

"*Big Dipper dips deeper 'n' Little—NOOOOOO!*" sang the cast.

"*Lunaverse's Got Talent, idle moon, mighty mooooon!*" sang Dazz.

"*Lunaverse's Got Talent, idle moon, mighty—WAAAAA!*" sang the cast.

The turbulence disappeared as fast as it had come. Hanazuki heaved a sigh of relief and loosened her grip on the steering wheel. Suddenly, Lavender was beside her, tugging at her skirt. "Momen bah," he whispered.

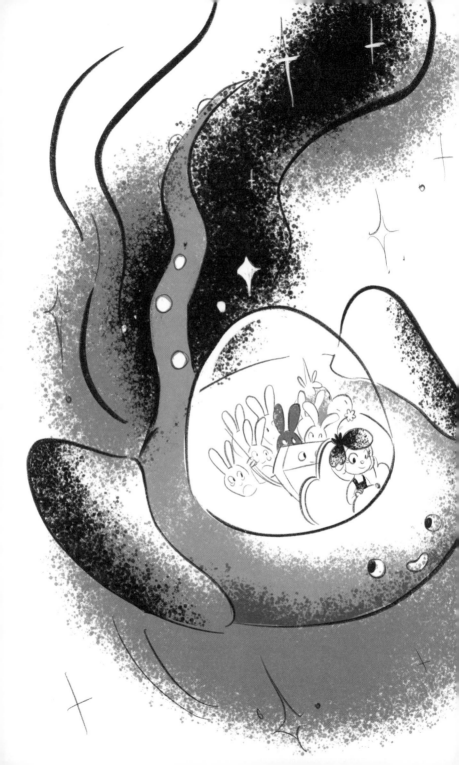

"A bad omen?" Hanazuki asked warily, wishing she could spend just a few minutes basking in the wowness of their survival. "You think the rocky travel means something bad is going to happen?"

Lavender shrugged, on the verge of tears.

"Aw, Lav. It's OK." Hanazuki didn't know much about bad omens, but she did know someone who knew lots about show business. "Hey, Dazz," she said, waving him into the conversation. "Isn't there something creatures say about rocky dress rehearsals?"

"Oh, sure," Dazz said. "A rocky dress rehearsal means a stellar opening night."

"Yee zoo boo?" asked Lav, a gleam of hope in his eyes.

Dazz nodded. "If this is our rocky start, then our act is going to rock!"

Hanazuki didn't know if Dazz was trying to make Lavender feel better or if that was the actual industry standard. Either way, she dug his interpretation. "Keep your eye on the grand prize, little guy," she told Lavender, tossing him onto her lap. "You think you can do that?"

"Gee pee," he sheepishly agreed, helping steer the spacesurfer.

Dazz went back to leading vocal warm-ups. Hanazuki joined in singing so that Lavender would feel comfortable joining in, too. Then, adrenaline pumping, she stepped on the gas.

CHAPTER FIVE

CELEBRITY MOON

H oly spaceballs," Hanazuki mumbled to herself as she and her friends exited the spacesurfer on Celebrity Moon. It was unlike anything she'd ever seen. Unlike anything she'd ever imagined. Unlike anything she could have possibly dreamed of!

The green grass glowed. The walking paths were mirrored. Glass pyramids lined the paths. Mounted on top of the pyramids were bowls of creams, lotions, soaps, and mints. In the fields behind them, cellophane-wrapped rose bunches were growing from glittery stalks. Lavish scarecrows were dressed in high-fashion gowns and jewelry. Open-toed high heels formed

"waterslides" into gold and silver swirl lakes. The Mouth Portals' lips were smothered in sparkly gloss. Gold trinkets—keys and doorknobs and lockets and cufflinks—floated around the atmosphere. Diamond studs twinkled in the sky. The clouds were strings of pearls. Everything was flashy. Everything was fashionable. Everything screamed CELEBRITY.

Kiazuki and Maroshi met Hanazuki and Lavender, and the four of them stumbled around, taking in the unchartered territory with amazement.

"Sick, dude!" Maroshi said, swiping at a floating gold bow tie. "Kiyoshi would get a kick out of this!"

"Um, wait," Hanazuki said. "Where *is* Kiyoshi?"

Kiazuki shrugged. "Maybe he's on his own moon."

"Why would he be there?" Hanazuki asked. "He was rehearsing on my moon."

"He is using the Little 'Corns and lots of magic,"

Maroshi replied. "I bet he had to make a pit stop to refuel or get mad props."

"Maybe," Hanazuki said as her friends raced ahead. She looked at Lavender, afraid he'd remind her about the bad omen, but he was all sparkly-eyed staring at an enormous gold trophy.

"Well hello, shiny bro," Maroshi said to it.

"This is, like, the big version of our treasures," Kiazuki said.

"There's more of them," Maroshi said, surfing ahead. "Every path has a different trophy. They're like street signs!"

"Street signs?" Hanazuki asked.

"Yeah, they tell you where you're at," Maroshi explained. "So I can be like, 'Hanazuki, meet me at the corner of Gold Unicorn Trophy and Silver Swan Trophy.'"

"Well, that's awesome."

"Is that ice?!" Kiazuki blurted out, pointing to a sculpture of a Treasure Tree. Zikoro was licking it, and his tongue stuck a little each time.

"*Brrr*, it is!" Hanazuki said, feeling its trunk. "But you know what I don't see? Actual Treasure Trees."

"That's probably 'cause they've got 'em all packaged up for the winner," Maroshi said.

"The winner being me," Kiazuki added.

Hanazuki ignored her. "I didn't realize that Celebrity Moon was giving away *all* of their trees. I assumed they were just giving away their extra ones since they have so many."

"What do you care?" Kiazuki asked.

"Well, without trees, how is the moon going to protect itself from the Big Bad?"

"I bet fancy trophies repel the Big Bad, too."

"*Maaaybe*?" This time when she looked at Lavender, he gave her a *Something's fishy* look back.

But before she could get into it, Dazzlessence was chasséing toward them and then pliéd to a halt. "Hey, H!" he said, panting. "I've been looking all over for you! Our call time was five minutes ago."

Hanazuki's heart dropped. "Oh, no! I totally lost track of time. Where do we go?"

"Back where we landed, there are gold arrows on a glittery, red moon-rock road. Below those gold arrows, it reads: 'Follow the Red Carpet to Lunaverse's Got Talent.'"

"'Red carpet'?" Kiazuki said. "Swoon."

"You're tellin' me," Dazz said, fanning himself. "This moon is my dream moon."

Hanazuki, Lavender, Dazz, and her Moonflower friends gathered their teams and sprinted along the road until they arrived at a red velvet curtain. Above it was a blinking gold sign that read RIGHT THIS WAY, MOONFLOWERS. Hanazuki whizzed through the curtain opening and then stopped short to soak it in.

The backstage area was enormous and open, a sea of Moonflowers and their alterlings, warming up, ironing costumes, and doing hair and makeup. One Moonflower was jumping on a trampoline, while her catlike alterlings spat up hair balls for her to juggle. Another Moonflower was singing a folk song about craters, while her mini mooselike alterlings accompanied her on the harmonica. Another Moonflower, in a lab coat, was coaching his froglike alterlings to bottle up their burps.

"Wel-come," said a robotic voice.

Hanazuki turned around and there was, in fact, a robot. Its face was a video camera. "Uh, hi there, robot camera creature."

"Please do not ad-dress me di-rect-ly. I'm live-streaming for our audience."

"Your Celebrity Moon audience is watching me right now?!"

"Please do not ad-dress me di-rect-ly," it repeated. "I'm live-streaming for our audience." The video camera zoomed in so close, the lens was practically touching Hanazuki's face.

"Not sure that's my best angle."

It zoomed back out and then rolled away. There were more robots zipping around backstage. Some of them had video cameras for faces, others had boxy heads and two metal eyes and two metal ears and one metal nose and one metal mouth.

Hanazuki flagged down the closest non-video-camera bot. "Hi! I'm Hanazuki. Can I check in?"

The robot flashed a gold-toothed smile. "You got it! Your quest to be a star isn't far!"

"Oh, thank you! I was worried because we're a little late. Do you know where my team is in the running order?"

The robot closed its mouth and began to zip away.

"Wait! Are we first? Last? Somewhere in the middle?"

"You got it!" a second bot replied in the exact same tone. "Your quest to be a star isn't far!"

"Cool, thanks," Hanazuki said. "But I'm curious about the order?"

The robot closed its mouth and zipped away. "You got it!" a third bot replied in the exact same tone. "Your quest to be a star isn't far!" Then that robot closed its mouth and zipped away, too.

"Well, that's weirder than weird," Hanazuki mumbled. She figured if she couldn't get any information from the bot attendants, she might as well start rehearsing. She carved out a spot for her team to run their act, but it was hard for them to focus with Kiazuki beside them, reviewing her hip-hop duet with Zikoro. She wiggled her hips while Zikoro stood on his hind legs and wiggled his bum. When she clapped, he sprang into her arms. When she snapped, he played patty-cake with her. But then Wanderer joined them and Zikoro went ballistic, trying to chase him up an ice sculpture.

"Wanderer, we're in the middle of our biggest surfing trick," Maroshi reminded him, pointing to the rest of the Flochi, who were doing in-sync water aerobics in a silver fountain filled with sparkling water.

Hanazuki turned her focus back to her team. "Let's run it again!" she called. But no one moved. Sleepy Unicorn was so hopped up on orange-fruit-juice tablets, he was shaking in the corner. Dazz was stuck in a split, saying, "Ow. Leg cramp. Ow." Lavender was frantically marking everyone's places in a color-coordinated binder. Without Green to run lights, Pink didn't know where to spotlight. Teal was stitching up a major tear in Purple's costume. Yellow, Orange, and Blue were shimmying into each other. Lime Green was trying not to hyperventilate.

Before Hanazuki could rein in her team, she got distracted by a familiar voice, saying, "Yaaaas, gurl. Get it. I'm the gurl. I'm getting it." Hanazuki turned around to see Miyumi on top of her crystal spaceboard. She was more bejeweled than normal—even her eyelashes had jewels on them! Her handbag Slooth, BB, was also extra bejeweled for the occasion, sporting a bejeweled collar, bejeweled footies, bejeweled sunglasses, and a bejeweled trucker hat. "And a me, a you, a Mi-yu-mi." Miyumi burst out in auto-tuned glitzy polka pop. Her Slooths sang backup, "*Yaaas, girl, yaaas.*" They body-rolled at the start of every verse, so slowly that their spines only straightened by the chorus.

Hanazuki wiped her palms on her skirt. She was starting to get nervous. Her team was awesome, but so was everybody else's team. All of the acts were so different! What if the celebrity judge was a huge fan of polka pop? What if they were a surf lover? What if they took hip-hop classes to stay in shape? Lunaverse's Got Talent could easily go to any Moonflower here!

Hanazuki dragged her team to an extraquiet corner, determined to focus them. "We've come so far, guys. Let's not let anything get in the way, OK? In *three, two, one*—!"

Before Hanazuki could call "Action!" a new Moonflower with pink bleached hair tips and a pink rattail strutted up to Sleepy Unicorn and asked, "Are you a Moonflower or a horse?"

"Neither," Sleepy said.

"Lavender, keep the rehearsal going," Hanazuki

instructed, marching up to the Moonflower. "Hiya! We're running our act. Do you think you can give us some room?"

The Moonflower made a duck face and pointed at Sleepy. "Are you this cow's mother?"

"Do you mean unicorn?" Hanazuki asked.

"So you're a mama-corn?"

"No, I'm a Moonflower."

The Moonflower looked Hanazuki up and down, and so she did the same to him. He was wearing a pleather jacket and pleather fringed leggings and furry boots with springs at the bottom. "What's your costume?" she asked. "It's so unique."

"Costume?!" he scoffed. "Darling, this ain't no costume. When you're as high fashion as I am, you've got to be ready to be photographed and interviewed and paid to be a sponsor for a brand at any moment."

"Bran? The cereal?"

The Moonflower rolled his eyes so hard, they got stuck in the back of his head. He sneezed, and they bobbed back to normal. "Honeycakes, do you not recognize me? I'm all over the network. I model for Crater Skate Parks and Moon Rock Guitars." He whistled and his alterlings—prissy pets with the faces of Pomeranians and the bodies of fireflies—flocked to his outstretched arms. They yapped at Hanazuki, baring miniature fangs. "These are my Hotaru. They're usually not so fond of other Moonflowers, but they seem to adore you. Aren't they precious?"

"'Precious' isn't the first word that comes to mind."

"But it's the second word, I bet." He snuggled them. "I wuv you, I wuv your poofy faces and bright-light bodies, my delicious snacks."

"I'm Hanazuki, by the way," Hanazuki said, extending her hand.

"I'm Hoshi. It means 'star.'" Instead of shaking, he squeezed a glob of hand sanitizer into her palm.

Confused, she just rubbed it in. "Well, nice

meeting you, Hoshi. Time to get back to my team. So, yeah. Again, if you can rehearse elsewhere, that would be very much appreciated."

Hanazuki stepped aside to tend to her rehearsal when Maroshi surfed in. "Hey, you're Hoshi, right?" he called, kicking up his spaceboard and catching it in a sack on his back. "You're the Crater Skate Park dude, right?"

Hoshi flipped his rattail. "Who's asking?"

"Uh, me. Maroshi. Wassup?"

"The blessed sky." Hoshi applied black wax to his lips and smacked them together. "Want to see a preview of my act? I don't just go around performing for free, but since you're a megafan, it's the proper thing to do."

"Right on!"

By now, Hanazuki had taken the reins back from Lavender and was running the act's double-speed tap dance finale. But behind them, a gold runway unraveled at Hoshi's feet. She watched as he bounce-strutted to the end of it, uncomfortably close to where her team was rehearsing. He slipped his Hotaru's collars around his ankle and spun them around in a 360-degree rotation while skipping over them with his other foot. The Hotaru lit up, creating a halo at his feet. "You think I'm done, don't you?" he asked the crowd.

"Are you?" Maroshi asked.

"Hoshi is never done," he said, whipping out a flag from his back pocket and performing an interpretative flag dance. "He will win Lunaverse's Got Talent and every competition after Lunaverse's Got Talent. His agent said so."

"Who's your agent?"

"Let's not get into it. It's tacky."

Hanazuki couldn't believe it. Could this Moonflower be any more full of himself? How was Maroshi such a fan? Also, could he get out of her team's space so they could practice? Unable to focus, they were starting to tap offbeat! Unable to focus on directing, she couldn't get them back on track!

Hoshi laid down his flag. "I know you probably want my autograph, Maroshi—"

"Could be cool."

"—but I prefer to give your spaceboard a ride and, instead, leave my artistic mark."

Hoshi was giving the spaceboard a go, striking model poses midair, when Kiazuki strutted over to Hanazuki. "Who is this bragalicious Moonflower?" she asked.

"His name is Hoshi, and, apparently, Maroshi's obsessed with him." Hanazuki sighed, watching her team tap so out of sync, it sounded like a stampede of high heels. She called to the Moonflower guys, "You know what would be really fun? Doing all your surfing tricks waaaaaay over there."

"What's that, Hanazuki?" Hoshi asked. "You don't think your team stands a chance against us?" He swooped down on the spaceboard and gave Maroshi a backward high five.

"Pfff," Kiazuki said. "She said she'll share her trees with you when she wins."

"Booyah!" Hanazuki cried, giving Kiazuki a backward high ten.

Just then, a formal, robotic voice blasted down from the sky. "Good day, Moonflowers from moons a-cross the gal-ax-y. Thank you for being here to-day for Lunaverse's Got Talent, and break legs during your performances. The show will be-gin in approx-i-mately one minute. Please listen as I call Moonflowers and their teams to the stage. After each act, the teams will ex-it through the purple cur-tain to the post-performance wing. First up is Miyumi and her Slooths."

One minute! That's it? Hanazuki launched her team into a speed-through of their act. Meanwhile, Miyumi whipped her topknotted ponytail around, and glittery perfume flew from her hair. "That's my aura, gurl," she said to no one in particular. Then it was time, and she and BB pranced through a purple velvet curtain with a sign over it that read THE STAGE. The rest of her Slooths followed so slowly that it was likely

Miyumi would finish performing before they'd made it through.

Hanazuki tried to keep her team rehearsing—running through dance moves, perfecting the timing, staying in sync—but it was even harder to focus as their time to perform came closer and closer. The robotic sky voice continued to call Moonflower after Moonflower after Moonflower. The waiting area was slowly clearing, and before she knew it, there were only three teams left!

"Hoshi and his Hotarus are up," the voice announced. "Kiazuki and Zikoro are next."

That means we're last! The grand finale! Hanazuki and her team stood by the purple curtain and listened in on Hoshi's act. She heard the *cree-craw cree-craw* of his springy moonshoes. She heard the *dubdubdubdub* of the Hotarus swinging around his ankle. She heard the *whoosh-swoosh* of his flag flapping in the air. And then, she heard the audience scream. Was the celebrity judge loving Hoshi's act? Was the live-streamed audience giving him a standing O?

"Kiazuki, you're up," the voice announced. "Hanazuki and her Hemka, Diamond, and Unicorn, you're next."

Hanazuki's heart raced as she listened to Zikoro's barking and Kiazuki's dancing feet, followed by uproarious applause. She briskly waved her team into a tight huddle. "We've got this. Hands in. 'Trees for life' on three! *One, two*—"

"Don't do it," Kiazuki hissed, suddenly popping her head out from behind the curtain.

"Huh?" Hanazuki asked. "Don't do what?"

"Everybody's been coming onstage with all this confidence, but exiting like flat balloons. The celebrity judge hasn't even shown himself. And sure—the audience screamed that I'm 'famous as fly,' but they weren't even there. At best, they were live-streamed on massive screens from outside the theater."

Hanazuki eyed Kiazuki with suspicion. Was this her Moonflower sister's way of sabotaging her?

"I'm serious, Hanazuki—don't do it."

"Last but not least," the voice beckoned. "Dazz, er, Hanazuki, your team is up."

"Sorry, Kiazuki," Hanazuki said. "We've come too far. Nobody nor nothing can stop us." Kiazuki huffed and then slipped back behind the curtain into the postperformance wing, while Hanazuki waved her team through to the stage. *We've got this*, she told herself as they took their places. *We'll get an even bigger and better reaction than all the teams before us. We're going to work together and make galactic history. We're taking home those trees!* With seconds to spare, she stuck her head out from the wings to check out the moon creatures on these so-called screens. They didn't seem like creatures, more like trophies with faces. At the foot of the stage was a judge's chair, but it was facing backward. It *was* kind of creepy.

Still, she could handle creepy. She and her team had overcome far worse!

The robotic voice continued, "All performers come out on-to the bal-co-ny and watch. I re-peat, all performers come out on-to the bal-co-ny and watch."

Hanazuki's stomach flipped with excitement. All the Moonflowers and their teams were being brought into the audience to cheer her team on! Was it because they were the final act? Or because everyone already knew how incredible they'd be? As the performers trickled into the balcony, the Hemka lit up. Sleepy raised his hooves, posing like a star. Dazz blew kisses.

Suddenly, a big red light at the back of the audience flicked green. It was go time!

Lavender, who was beside Hanazuki in the wings, cued Sleepy with an ear wave. He began, "*To be or not to be!*" The stage mics picked up his voice, and he sounded incredibly bold. Like a professional actor, even! The Hemka hopped in place, clapping their ears above their heads. Blue was crying tears of joy. Orange was hopping higher than he'd ever hopped before. Yellow's smile was as big as his face. Purple was closing his eyes, bravely overcoming what appeared to be the onset of stage fright.

Sleepy Unicorn moved into the Running Unicorn. Faster, faster. He danced out of the spotlight, coming down onto a floor mic.

BOOOOOOM! Vibrations tore across the stage and into the audience. Confused, Blue cried harder. Orange stopped hopping. Yellow's smile faded. Purple's eyes shot open, and he beat his chest, re-tearing his costume.

The judge's chair throbbed, and all of a sudden, small black objects from the seat plummeted to the floor. Lime Green began shrieking backstage. Teal threw his ears over Lime Green's mouth. Hanazuki leaped onstage to investigate, and the crowd began to hiss, "Step back, Moonflower! Step back!"

The robotic voice sounded, "Au-di-ence, throw the tomatoes, now!"

Tomatoes? Hanazuki thought. There were confused murmurs coming from the balcony, and then some shouting, washed out by the hissing of the on-screen Celebrity Moon creatures.

Hanazuki scrambled to the edge of the stage as black objects of all shapes and sizes continued to drop from the judge's chair. The hissing turned into boos as tomatoes rained down from the fly loft onto the stage.

Sleepy and most of the Hemka shielded their heads. Orange opened his mouth and tried to catch the tomatoes as they splattered onto his face. Dazzlessence, tomato-splattered and mortified, dove off the stage and spun the judge's chair around. "*It's a fake judge!*" he sang.

Hanazuki gasped. Fake was right. The celebrity judge was just a moon creature made of rotting black treasure fruit. His eyes, ears, hair, body, arms, and legs—all fruit!

Sleepy Unicorn pointed to a green velvet curtain at the back of the house. On it was a sign that read GRAND PRIZE, HA! "That doesn't sound suspicious at all," he said sarcastically.

Hanazuki dashed to the back of the house and pulled the curtain aside. There were trees, all right. *Wilting black Treasure Trees*. All of a sudden, the screens went staticky. The cameras recording for the brain networks blinked from green to red and then powered off. Sirens wailed. A robotic announcement kicked in over it: "Dis-quali-fied. Dis-quali-fied. Lunaverse's Got Talent is now over. Ha, ha, Dazzlessence Jones. Worst. Performance. Ever. Everybody please return to your moons. Celebrity Moon is not responsible for any loss of time, energy, effort, or mooney. Goodbye."

CHAPTER SIX

SCAMMED!

We've got to get out of here," Hanazuki said to her team as they huddled backstage wearing space blankets, paralyzed in shock. "Whatever just happened—that was targeted at *us*."

"*At meeeeeeeee*," Dazz cry-sang.

The sirens had stopped, the fancy lights had gone dark, the robots had short-circuited, and an eerie silence now crept across the theater. Moonflowers left the balcony and filtered onstage in massive confusion. Some dropped their tomatoes—or smashed them in anger—demanding that the Celebrity Moon creatures, wherever they were, give them an explanation.

Others were running to their spacesurfers, to their moons, afraid they'd be targeted next.

"I'm humiliated," Hoshi said. "I'm the galaxy's brightest star, and I flew all this way for nothing."

"You're preaching to the choir," Miyumi told him. "I spent eleven hours bejeweling my body. I normally spend seven."

Before she could respond, Kiazuki was shaking Hanazuki by the shoulders. "See?! I told you something strange was going on!"

"Ugh, you're right. I know. This is totally a scam!"

"Yup. We've got to get off this moon this instant. We also need to figure out what happened, who was behind it, and why."

"Roger that. Go ahead. I'll get my team moving."

"I'll meet you back at the parking lot," Kiazuki said. "Hurry!" Keeping a watchful eye, she hurried after Zikoro, and the rest of the Moonflowers and their teams followed.

Hanazuki gave her full attention to her team. Blue was sobbing, but the rest of them were silent.

"Hey, guys," she said softly. "I know this whole thing is confusing and heartbreaking and weird in all the worst ways, but we've got to get back to our moon. I just have a feeling that whatever this was, it isn't over."

Dazz flicked a tomato skin from his shoulder and heaved a sad sigh. "*This is terrible*," he sang. "All our hard work and this is how we are treated? Also, why did they say *my* name? It's *your* team, Hanazuki."

"I have no idea." Hanazuki and her team began to move toward the parking lot. Before exiting through the curtain, she turned around to take in the black, lonely stage littered with smashed tomatoes and sequins. "Goodbye, Lunaverse's Got Talent," she whispered, before spotting Lavender as he burst from the wings, doing the most amazing gymnastics she'd ever seen. Cartwheels! Handsprings! Flips! Somersaults! Earstands! Headstands! Split leaps! Oh, the talent! "Lav, you're absolutely INCREDIBLE!" she cried.

Lavender shrank out of an aerial.

"Aw, no!" Hanazuki said, rushing to him. "No need to be timid! You should have been performing that in our act all along!"

Lavender fell into Hanazuki's arms. "Na tee ree tal tal."

"What do you mean you're not reliable?"

"Nee fur giv hay loo."

Hanazuki snuggled him. "You wouldn't have made the team lose, Lav! You're scared of failing in front of others, and that feeling freezes you up. I get it. But trust me, you would have knocked it out of the park!"

Lavender blinked, and a tear slid from his eye. "Mah mez a fee joi."

"Performing brings you joy," Hanazuki repeated, wowed, then paused a moment. Her mind seemed to be performing its own mental gymnastics—thoughts flipped and bounced and flew across her mind and out of her mouth. "This whole time it's been about bringing our friends together to put on an amazing, winning show, but not once did I stop and think *why*? The why for you is that performing makes you feel amazing."

"Kee na za da," Lavender said, nodding as if he missed performing already.

Hanazuki felt her stomach flip with inspiration. "You know what, Lav? When this is all over, we're going to put on our own show. We can invite other Moonflowers to our moon to perform. There will be no winners or grand prize or anything, but any creature who wants to can express their talents and be a part of something extraordinary! You can do gymnastics if the inspiration strikes, but there will be no pressure either way!"

"Yoo zizza mitz!" Lavender blurted out, lighting up brighter than all of Hoshi's Hotaru combined.

"I thought you'd like that idea," Hanazuki said, smiling back. "We'll talk more back on our moon!" Lavender scissor-leaped ahead toward the spacesurfer, and Hanazuki did everything in her power to keep up. When they arrived, her team was already inside. Kiazuki and Zikoro had their spacesurfer's engine revving. Hoshi and Maroshi were on their spaceboards, preparing for takeoff.

"Sorry for keeping you waiting, Moonflowers," Hanazuki said as she and Lavender fastened themselves in. "Let's all get rocking." She watched Kiazuki, Hoshi, and Maroshi whisk into the air and then zoomed off into the atmosphere, too.

As they flew closer and closer to home, Hanazuki's worries started to set in. She still had no idea who had plotted the Lunaverse's Got Talent scam or why, which gave her a sinking feeling the worst had yet to come. What if she arrived home to wilting black Treasure Trees? What if the Celebrity Moon creatures had trespassed onto her moon for a Lunaverse's Got Talent winner of their own? What if the celebrity judge was real and awaiting her return, armed with hundreds of tomatoes? Thousands of tomatoes? What if Red and Green and Doughy and Chicken Plant and maybe even Basal were in danger?

She took a deep breath to calm her nerves, but she couldn't turn off her mind. It was being pulled in a million different directions. It didn't help that the Hemka were bickering over the front seat, shoving and shape-shifting and restraining one another with seat belts. Dazz had ripped off his dance pants and was crying, "I don't shine at all when I'm soaked in tomatoes! Who wants my dance pants? Not me!"

Sleepy slowly raised a hoof, finally coming down from his orange-tablet buzz. "I like those pants, Dazz. If I fold them, I can use them as a neck pillow." Dazz threw the pants at Sleepy, who placed them under his neck and instantly fell asleep. The Hemka screamed as he toppled over, nearly crushing them.

As Hanazuki steered, she tried her best to keep it together. The whole point of Lunaverse's Got Talent was to bring her friends together as a team, and after hurdling over so many obstacles, they might just be about to face their biggest obstacle yet. Could they handle it?

CHAPTER SEVEN

A TWIST OF EVENTS

OOOOOOOOO!"

From inside her hovering spacesurfer, Hanazuki and her friends watched with horror as Twisted Unicorn (Sleepy Unicorn's evil brother) and Randy (Dazzlessence's disgruntled cousin) ransacked her moon.

"*This can't be happening!*" Dazz sang angrily as they stealthily landed. "Randy? That dude? He's behind this? Let me get out. Let me tear him in two!"

The Hemka threw themselves over Dazz's mouth to quiet him. Meanwhile, Sleepy Unicorn, who should have been panicking, was fast asleep. Hanazuki went to wake him, when she heard a knock. "You scared me!" she gasped at Kiazuki, rolling down the window.

"I scared you?" Kiazuki whispered. "I'm freaking out! We were scammed and fell for it, Maroshi and Hoshi are spaceboarding slower than moon molasses, and now this Twisted dude and diamond thing are trying to take over your moon!"

Dazzlessence scoffed. "Randy's not a diamond. He's a cubic zirconia. Which, in case you don't know your jewels, means that he's *faaaaaake*."

"Well, he is *truthfully* damaging your home," Kiazuki said.

"On it," Hanazuki said with as much confidence as she could muster. "I'm sure Maroshi and Hoshi will be here soon, but we've got to act now. Hemka, pinch Sleepy awake. Then, quickly and quietly follow me." The Hemka obeyed, and she led her friends through the moonweeds, where they could more clearly see Twisted working his evil magic.

"Oh, no, look!" Kiazuki said, pointing at Kiyoshi, who was captured in a floating bubble.

He cried, "Leave me alone! Leave us all alone! This isn't your moon!"

"This isn't your moon either, you useless Moonflower," Twisted snarled.

"Good one, T," Randy said, offering a high five. Twisted slapped his arm down.

"I'm useful," Kiyoshi fought back. "I can see stuff in the black Treasure Tree leaves!"

"Like what?" Randy asked.

"Like the past, present, and future."

"Big whoop," Twisted said. "Past—I wasn't here. Present—I'm here. Future—I'm helping Randy take over this moon."

"Zing!!!" Randy said, then bragged, "I totally tricked my cousin. I set up this crazy contest knowing he'd throw his whole egotistical self into it, and then just when he was led to believe that his team was the grand finale, so sparkly they might just win—*BAM!* Tomatoes! A booing live audience!

A hissing virtual audience! All the elements of a terrible, soul-crushing, mortifying, I'll-never-do-this-again performance! Wish you could have been there. Wish *I* could have been there! Ha!"

Hanazuki felt her skin crawl. "Well, he put a lot of effort into being a jerk. And no, no, poor Kiyoshi," she mumbled. "We've got to help him."

"Do you see that?" Kiazuki said, now pointing at a bubble with trapped space spam. "I bet Kiyoshi was trying to warn us of Twisted and Randy's takeover, but the message never made it off the moon."

Hanazuki looked at Dazz. "Why does Randy want to take over my moon?!"

"Who knows? I'm not my inferior cousin's keeper!" Dazz began to pace. "I can't believe Randy is pulling this off. Randy has never pulled anything off! He's usually all disgruntle, no action." He sped up. "How'd he get Twisted on his side? How'd he get Twisted to do his dirty work?! It doesn't make any sense!"

"Did someone say, 'Twisted?'" Sleepy drawled, suddenly conscious. He peered through the moonweeds and yelped. "That's my brother! He's forcing the Little Unicorns to do heavy labor. Look! They're picking and destroying all the treasure fruit! Except the red ones. That's weird. I guess growing up, he liked wearing red sweaters. Especially around the holidays. Is it the holiday season?"

Kiazuki slapped her hand over Sleepy's mouth. "*Shhhhhhhhhhhhhhhhh!*"

"I think I know what's happening," Hanazuki whispered. "The last time Twisted attacked my moon, he was defeated by the strength of his own emotions. Remember? We threw treasure fruit at him, and that made him feel stuff, like, fifty times more powerfully."

"My brother needs to get in touch with his softer feelings," Sleepy said.

"For sure. But right now, he's probably thinking that rage, feistiness, gruffness, and defiance are the only feelings he can use to his advantage." Hanazuki watched the Little Unicorns zap a pink Treasure Tree to death. Black hearts floated down from its branches. Twisted laughed, then cracked open a red treasure fruit and slurped its juice. His muscles throbbed. He tore down a lime-green Treasure Tree, exposing a floating bubble with Red Hemka and Green Hemka trapped inside. Red was trying to fry the bubble with the steam flying out of his ears. Green was doing yoga.

"No, no, no, no," Hanazuki said.

"I guess creatures handle stress differently," Sleepy remarked.

"We've got to get them out of there. Come on!"

Hanazuki led the way through the moonweeds and around Talking Pyramid, who was gagged with at least a dozen socks. "Duck!" she called, as Twisted and Randy circled back. She and her friends threw themselves behind a row of bushes. After Twisted and Randy passed, Hanazuki slowly peered over it. Red and Green were probably only fifty paces away! Even closer was Doughy Bunington, tied to a pink Treasure Tree and whimpering for scones.

Hanazuki ducked back down. "OK, I think I've found a way," she told her friends, "but we've got to crawl. Stay low!" She led them around the bushes, along a yellow moon-rock road, and inside a small pink Treasure Tree grove. Randy was there, supervising the mass destruction of all things pink. Basal Ganglia was taunting him from a locked cage on the ground.

"One could say that I'm the free one, and you're in a cage," he said. "Makes sense. Since you're my subject."

"I'm not your subject," Randy protested. "You're MY subject."

"Oh, dandy Randy. That's hysterical. *Mwah ha ha ha!*"

"Stop evil laughing! I'm the evil one. *Mwee hee hee hee!*"

The two of them evil-laughed over each other,

louder and louder, until Randy broke into a coughing fit and couldn't evil-laugh any longer.

"Let me tell you about the moon's greatest resources, Randy," Basal said. "Under Rainbow Swirl Lake is an underwater tunnel system. But only I have the key."

"Where? How?" Randy asked. "You don't have arms!"

"I have lobes, you pathetic pawn-shop sheriff."

"Twisted, tell him to stop making fun of me!" Randy whined.

"Stop," Twisted said flatly.

"I'd offer you the key," Basal went on taunting, "but I'm not sure it's safe with you. After all, you're vulnerable to scratches."

"*You're* vulnerable to scratches!"

"Of course I am. I'm a brain. *BWAHAHAHA-HAHAHA!*"

"*AAAAARG!*" Randy cried. "Twisted, make Basal Ganglia give me the key!"

"There is no key because there is no tunnel," Twisted told him. "You're a nitwit."

"A nitty witty bitty nitwit indeed," Basal said, grinning.

"I'm torn," Dazz whispered to Kiazuki. "I'm enjoying watching Basal rip into Randy, but I also feel comforted with Basal in a cage."

"Does it matter?" Kiazuki whispered back. "It's not like Basal can move on his own."

"Touché."

"Focus!" Hanazuki said. "Galactic gosh, I knew this would happen. I knew I should have trusted my instincts. But Dazz—you really were acting so controlling. I didn't know how to say no to you!"

Dazz winced. "I don't have an excuse, but I do have a reason."

"Well, when we're not in crisis mode, I'd love to hear it."

"Uhhh, what's going on?" Kiazuki asked.

"Sleepy had a dream, and I learned that Randy has it out for Dazz," Hanazuki answered quickly.

"I thought he might be involved in this somehow. I should have pulled the plug on our competing before we'd left for Celebrity Moon."

"Seriously?" Kiazuki said. "What about Twisted? Did you think he'd be involved in this mess, too?"

"Nope," Hanazuki replied. "He's the wild card."

"Out of SIGHT, out of MIND!" Randy suddenly exclaimed, throwing a cloth over Basal Ganglia's cage. Then, he threw an arm over Twisted Unicorn's shoulder. "Thanks so much for helping me make my mark on this moon." He sang, "*Oh, I just can't wait to be sheriff!*"

"I don't care what you are," Twisted sneered, removing Randy's arm like it was a used tissue, "as long as you uphold your end of the bargain."

"Good thing I'm a bargain upholder!" Randy laughed and then shouted toward the sky, "I'm sheriff now! I dare you to come back and try to take the reins from me, you undazzling dinosaur!"

"Is he shouting at me?" Dazz asked. "Did he just call me *undazzling*?!"

"And a dinosaur," Sleepy said.

"After this, you've got my forever loyalty," Randy went on to Twisted. "I'll run a tight ship on this moon under your intergalactic supervision and make sure your brother stays in check."

Sleepy Unicorn cocked an eyebrow. "Stays in whaaaat now?"

"Whatever you need," Randy said to Twisted, "I'm the loyal diamond for the job."

"'Diamond'?" Dazz repeated. "Is he seriously posing as a DIAMOND now?!" His voice lurched out of a whisper. "I am straight-up MAD and OFFENDED. That's it, Randy Jones! *You're asking for a SPARKLE OFFFFFFF!*"

Randy paused like a synthetic jewel in headlights. "Did you hear something, Twisted?"

Hanazuki and her friends froze in terror. Dazz wasn't terrified—just furious—but he froze in solidarity.

Twisted grumbled to Randy, "I hear YOU, and that's more than my ears can handle." He trotted off toward a lime-green Treasure Tree grove. "You are one minute away from intolerable, Randy Jones."

"So I'm tolerable for a whole minute more? Yowza!" Randy jumped for joy, then followed Twisted toward the grove.

Hanazuki heaved a sigh of relief. "All right, friends," she said, "let's figure out the—NO, NOT YET!"

Without any warning, Purple Hemka and Yellow Hemka began racing toward Red Hemka and Green Hemka. In a flash, Sleepy Unicorn downed the rest of his mega-energy tablets and zapped Purple and Yellow back to the group. "Yaaaaaaaa!" they cried, teasing out like cotton balls.

"Thanks, Sleepy," Hanazuki said, patting the rogue Hemka back to normal. "C'mon, everybody. We need to be smart about this or we'll get ourselves captured, too."

"Fine. Smart ideas, go," Kiazuki said.

Hanazuki bit her lip and tried to think clearly. How could she rescue her friends and also take Randy and Twisted down? She needed a secret weapon. But considering how sparse pink and yellow and lime-green and green and lavender treasure fruit now were, what were they supposed to do? *Wait . . .* She looked at creative, talented Lavender and felt a rush of inspiration from her head to her toes. "I got it, I got it, I got it!" she cried.

"Wanna share?" Kiazuki pressed. "This whole thing's kinda time-sensitive."

"Lav, what we were talking about earlier on Celebrity Moon—doing it under these circumstances wasn't quite what I had in mind, but I think it might just be the thing we *all* need."

Everybody looked at Lavender Hemka, who was staring at Little Dreamer, who was zipping around the sky, unperturbed, in a gorilla onesie with a microphone print on the hood.

Lavender took a moment and then slowly faced Hanazuki. His eyes were as wide as his smile. "Ga ga zee la la loo!" He quietly fell into a backbend and then launched into the air, throwing everybody into a curious *Wait, what is happening?* state.

Except for Hanazuki. She knew exactly what was up. Together, they had a plan.

CHAPTER EIGHT

SPARKLE OFF

So, what do you think?" Hanazuki asked, having just explained the plan. She and Lavender gripped hands, twitching with anticipation.

"*Let me get this straight*," Dazzlessence sang. "You want us to surprise attack Randy and Twisted Unicorn with a *show*?"

"Guerrilla theater," Sleepy Unicorn said. "I love it."

"Exactly!" Hanazuki said. "Forget treasure fruit! If we perform an act—one that's creative and brave and that shows off all of our talents combined, I bet it will trigger Twisted's true emotions. Plus, maybe Randy will soften, too. He'll see past Dazzlessence and his big ego—"

"Hey!" Dazz piped up.

"—and he'll see us working together as one great team. Randy can face his childhood conflict with Dazz—not through some elaborate scheme, but eye to eye!"

Kiazuki clapped silently. "Maybe Randy'll be so moved by the creativity of the show, he'll be inspired to perform, too."

"I dig it," Sleepy chimed in. "And this time, there will be no winners or losers."

"It'll just be about us—*all of us*—expressing our best talents." Suddenly realizing that there had to be more to the story, she narrowed her eyes at Dazz. "Why was Randy so mad at you? Was it really just jealousy, or—?"

"It's a *longish* story. How much time do we have?"

Just then, the Little Unicorns set a yellow Treasure Tree grove on fire. "No time at all!"

Hanazuki replied. "Fill me in later." She signaled Lavender, holding up one finger, two fingers, three fingers . . .

"PLAH-SA!!!" he called out.

Sleepy Unicorn burst out from behind the bush, aimed his horn at the yellow Treasure Tree grove, and fired magic. He quenched the fire, then broke into a rap. The Hemka hopped into plain sight and began shape-shifting at such great speeds, they appeared to be strobing. Dazzlessence shuffle-hopped over to Randy. "Well, hiya there, cuz."

Randy gasped in horror.

"I thought you said these losers were on Celebrity Moon," Twisted snarled.

"That's where they're supposed to be. It must have ended early."

Dazz lunged. "*Lookie here!*" he sang to Randy. "*Watch what we've got!*"

Purple Hemka and Pink Hemka harmonized, "*Ya ya ya-ya! Ya ya ya-ya!*" Sleepy's rap got faster. Dazzlessence did the Running Rock center

stage. The rest of the Hemka did the Running Hemka around him. Dazz hopped out of the circle and, one at a time, the Hemka hopped inside to perform their own special dance moves. Blue did the Onion Chop. Orange did the Ear Flop. Lime Green did the Nervous Shake. Teal did the Runway Strut. Yellow did the Jump 4 Joy.

"*Dancing, singing, cupcake icing, friendship,*

expression, teamwork!" Dazz sang. *"That's what it's all about!"*

"Ho, no!" Randy laughed. "Say that all you want! I know how embarrassed you must have been at Lunaverse's Got Talent. There's no way you're ever getting back on stage. Your love for performance has been shot through the heart. Your love for being front and center is finito. Your desire to be a star is dead!"

"Hate to break it to you, cuz," Dazz said, his feet feverishly tapping, "but you've destroyed nothing."

"Yeah, well, just you wait," Randy said. "There's only room for one star in this lunaverse, and that's Randy Jones."

Dazz kept dancing—tap, tap, ta-ta-tap. His moves got slicker, savvier, stronger.

"You'll never steal the spotlight again," Randy carried on, spinning on his upper girdle. "It's my time to shine—on THIS moon! So BACK OFF! I've got Twisted on my side! Right, Twisted?"

123

Hanazuki looked at Twisted, hoping to see a glimmer of emotion. A smile. A laugh. A tear. A twitch. But he was preoccupied with his own bulging figure, biting down on a red treasure fruit and examining his flexed muscles in the lake's reflection.

Dazz pirouetted. "So shine, baby."

"Huh?" said Randy.

"SHIIIIIIINE!"

Randy looked at his soot-coated body and then back at Dazz. "I am shining. Underneath."

"Uh-huh," Dazz said. "If you want to crush my love for performance, then I challenge you to crush me *in* performance. Onstage, not behind my back."

"If you think you're going to get me to dance—"

"What's the matter? Scared you'll lose?"

Suddenly, a gust of wind blew the cloth covering off Basal Ganglia's cage, and his jeering was loud and clear. "What a LOSER! Which unsightly jewel is named Randy? Oh! Oh! I know! A WANNABE!"

"Yeah, a WANNABE," repeated Dazz.

"You're the WANNABE, cuz," Randy shot back. "Why else would you try so desperately hard to be the star?"

"Me? Try hard?" Dazz scoffed, then sang, *"You're a sniveling NOTHING who needs a deranged, hopped-up UNICORN to do his dirty work!"*

Twisted smashed a yellow Treasure Tree. "What did you just sing?"

"SHUT IT, DAZZ," Randy piped up. "I'm not nothing! I'm EVERYTHING!"

"So prove it." Dazz paused in a plié. "Because I'm just getting started."

There was silence. The air was thick. All eyes were on the jewel cousins. Suddenly, Randy shifted his hip to the left. To the right. To the left. Dazz did the same. Randy waved his arms. Dazz sent his arms flailing. Randy did a handstand and then kicked his legs around in the air. Dazz did a one-armed handstand and then did an upside-down Running Diamond. Randy break-danced. Dazz break-danced faster. Randy sped up. Dazz danced double speed. Randy popped and locked. Dazz popped and locked and threw away the key. His legs started exploding. His body ebbed and dabbed and flowed and flexed and leaped and tumbled. "Oooh! I feel so good!!!!" he cried out.

Randy couldn't keep up. "You're trash!" he seethed between struggling breaths. "Dazz has no pizzazz!

"I have ALL THE PIZZAZZ!" Dazz sang. *"And you have some, too! Keep dancing! We're in this TOGETHER!"*

"Together?" Randy snorted. "Yeah, right!"

Hanazuki was mesmerized. Everyone was mesmerized! Even Twisted. Without realizing it, he'd retracted his magic bolt of lightning, and Kiyoshi, Red Hemka, and Green Hemka were free. Kiyoshi untied Doughy Bunington. Red Hemka pulled the socks out of Talking Pyramid's mouth. Oddly, Green Hemka continued to do yoga.

Hanazuki waved them over. "Here! With Kiazuki, Lavender, and me!"

Newly ungagged, Talking Pyramid began narrating the Sparkle Off like a sports announcer. "And Dazz is stepping left into a grapevine, while . . . Randy is doubled over, wheezing. Look at Dazz go! He's toe-touching like no other! Looks like Randy is about to face-plant. Chin up, Randy!"

Meanwhile, the Hemka had shape-shifted into a carousel. Little Dreamer was swooping through it. Sleepy was riding it and waving his hoof like royalty. It wasn't until he reached the top that Twisted Unicorn realized his hostages had escaped. He slammed his hoof to his horn.

"MY MAGIC! MY PRISONERS!!!"

No creature paid him any mind.

Dazz was twisting his heels into the moon earth. Randy was panting and trying to wiggle his bum.

The Hemka were shape-shifting into the petals of a sunflower. Sleepy became the flower's face.

"FINE," Twisted growled. "I'LL TAKE NEW PRISONERS!" He gobbled up seven red treasure fruit, pointed his horn at Dazz's dancing feet, and was about to strike when Little Dreamer led Maroshi and Hoshi to the scene. They surfed in, wearing matching pleather costumes.

"What up, what up," Maroshi called. "Hosh-Marosh in da moonhouse!"

CHAPTER NINE

A FAMILY FINALE

Hanazuki watched Maroshi and Hoshi surf between Randy and Dazz into Rainbow Swirl Lake. From the sky above, the Hotaru were lighting them in golden bursts. From the water below, the Flochi were creating a wave pool.

"Right on!" Maroshi called. "Keep them gnarly waves crashing!"

Maroshi and Hoshi duck-dove and popped up and trimmed. They bottom-turned and curved and kick-flipped. They performed foam climbs and tailslides and switch stances.

Randy's jaw was dropped. Twisted's eyes were glued. Everybody was speechless.

Still surfing, Hoshi whipped out a flag with his face on it. He waved it all around, through his legs, and around his back. Suddenly, a gust of wind blew it out of his hand and into the back of Maroshi's head. Maroshi wobbled. Hoshi wobbled, too. Then, a big wave crashed below them, and Maroshi went overboard. He fell into the lake with a *splash!* The Flochi dove to save him. The Hotaru tried to balance Hoshi, but their flashing golden light made him dizzy, and he fell overboard, too! He flailed around in Rainbow Swirl Lake, mascara running down his eyes. "EMERGENCY WARNING," he cried. "The pleather is water-resistant, but my makeup is not!"

Before Hanazuki could jump in to help, the Hemka shape-shifted into a massive fan. Within seconds, they had blown Hoshi and Maroshi out of the lake and dry. But they didn't stop there. The fan was running with such strength, it drove the water out of the lake and onto Twisted. He shrieked, then rung out his soaked body.

"THAT'S IT!" he howled. He spun, his horn aimed at the Hemka and Hoshi and Maroshi and Dazzlessence and Sleepy Unicorn and back at the Hemka. "I WILL END ALL OF YOU!"

Just then, Lavender swooped in, performing so many backflips so fast, he began spelling out a message.

"What are you doing, Lavender thing?" Twisted demanded, the electricity buzzing from his horn. "What are you spelling? STOP FLIPPING!"

But Lavender was unstoppable. Through his flips, he spelled out WE ARE FAMILY!

"No, we are NOT family!" Twisted roared. He threw red treasure fruit at Lavender, but the Hemka flipped out of the way. Instead, the fruit smashed Randy in the face.

"OWWWW!" Randy cried.

Meanwhile, Hoshi and Maroshi were back on the spaceboard and surfing through the crowd. "*Wally-wally-oooh!*" they cheered as Lavender added to his message: TOGETHER WE'RE BETTER!

Randy was covered in red juice. His arms were tired. His legs were sore. His insides were cramping. "Together we're NOT better," he wheezed.

"You sure about that?" Kiazuki asked. She held Zikoro's paws and they hip-hopped together.

Randy stared at them in awe. His chin quivered. His eyes went glassy. He sniffled and blinked, and then his tears spilled over. "I love watching Moonflowers dance with their alterlings! I've seen clips on the brain network but never live! It's stunning!"

Sleepy Unicorn began to rap: "*We. Are. Family. Family? Yes, family!*"

Randy began to rap along. "*We. Are. Family. Family? Yes, family!*"

Dazzlessence joined in. Kiyoshi, too. He reined in the Little Unicorns, and they shot glowing hearts into the black sky. The Hemka shape-shifted into fireworks and exploded through the hearts. Red! Orange! Yellow! Lime! Green! Blue! Teal! Purple! Pink!

Hanazuki began to twirl under the Hemkaworks! She caught sight of Randy—a sweaty, red, wet mess. He was laughing and crying and dancing and clapping. She grabbed his hands and twirled him, too. When Randy moved on to dance with Zikoro, Hanazuki stared at Lavender, still flipping, still promoting his "family" message. He was amazing. He was the most inspirational little guy she'd ever met.

Suddenly, Hanazuki felt a hand slip into hers.

"Remember our wager, H?" Kiazuki asked, her eyes on Lavender, too.

Hanazuki smiled. "Sure do. Whoever can grow a tree first through awesome inspiration and an awesome Lunaverse's Got Talent act wins a spa day."

"Check your pocket."

Hanazuki dug into her pocket and pulled out her treasure. It was glowing lavender. Kiazuki

pulled out hers. It was glowing lavender, too. "You thinking what I'm thinking?" Hanazuki asked.

"I think so!"

At the exact same moment, they threw down their original trophy treasures on either side of the stage and watched as two enormous, star-high, sparkly lavender Treasure Trees sprung up from the moon ground.

And then, all of a sudden, Sleepy Unicorn collapsed into a heavy slumber. His dream turned into a holographic projection!

Backstage at the talent show, Kid Sleepy Unicorn overheard Kid Dazz tell his Hollymoon manager, "If I win, I want to dedicate my award to my older cousin, Randy! He's so cool!"

The Hollymoon manager laughed in his face. "Absolutely not! Terrible for branding."

"Can he perform the encore with me?" Kid Dazz asked. "Pleeeeease! After all, we're family. Family sticks by one another's sides."

"Ugh, never say that again."

"We can burst out into a tap dance with top hats and canes!" Kid Dazz pressed. "It could be a magnificent end to a magnificent talent show!"

The Hollymoon manager got down on one knee and gave Dazz a cold, hard look. "Listen to me, Sparkle Kid—"

"They call me Jazzy Dazz," corrected Kid Dazz.

"*Jazzy Dazz*—when it comes to the spotlight, you've gotta be a moon shark in the water. You want backup dancers? Great. Keep 'em as backup—they can never share the flood of that shining solo light. Got it? If not, I'll drop you faster than a hot potato."

Kid Dazz peeked out at Kid Randy in the audience, wishing he didn't have to choose between his cousin and his career. He looked back at his Hollymoon manager and mumbled, "I got it."

"So, what life lesson have we learned, kid?"

"Be the star and nothing but the star?"

"Amen. From here on out, I'll make sure Randy

gets barred from every show in the galaxy. The spotlight's on you, Jazzy Dazz. So, give me forty percent of your earnings and also that shine!"

Sleepy Unicorn danced himself awake, and the projection disappeared. "What did I miss? We still dancing? *We. Are. Family!* Ooh! Rap it with me!" There were crickets. "Well, now I feel awkward."

"You ended up winning first place, Dazz," Randy said with wonder. "You wanted to dedicate it to me? Dance an encore with me? Even after everything I'd done to tear you down?"

"I did," Dazz said.

"That's beautiful," Randy whispered.

"*Beautiful is riiiight*," Dazz sang, wiping a single tear from his cheek.

"Hold up," Hanazuki said. "Is *that* why you were acting so crazy-controlling of the show, Dazz? Is *that* why you wouldn't let anyone else have the spotlight? Because of the bad influence of your kind of evil childhood manager?"

Dazz lowered his head in apology. "Yeah. After so many years of dance training under his management, his attitude burrowed inside of me. I didn't mean to be so bossy and selfish. I just forgot why I'd started dancing at all."

"Why *did* you start dancing?" Hanazuki asked.

"Because it gave me happy chills from my boots to my crown."

Hanazuki glanced at Lavender and felt her heart flutter with all the emotions—love, pride, forgiveness, joy, and most of all, inspiration. There was a joy to performing that Dazz and the rest of her team had neglected. No more! It was time to seek out and embrace those "happy chills" every step of the way!

"I'm sorry for choosing Mr. Hollymoon Manager over you," Dazz told Randy. "It wasn't too many years later that I put dancing aside to pursue different dreams—dreams of being a sheriff. I guess my guilt over it all—how I'd treated you—started to wear me down."

"I figured you were still dancing, Dazz," Randy said. "Still trying to block me from the business. I hadn't a sparkle of an idea."

"Yeah, we'd sort of fallen out of touch."

"I'm sorry I tried to sabotage you," Randy blurted out. "Then held a grudge for a very long time. Then set up an elaborate scam to humiliate you. Then tried to take over your moon."

The cousins stared at each other. Their shining bodies reflected off each other. "When you shine, I shine," they said together.

Twisted gagged. "Are you KIDDING me with this cheese?" he exclaimed. "SNAP OUT OF IT! You're feeling all the weak feelings you're NOT SUPPOSED TO FEEL! We had a deal. I help you, you help me—"

"We're a happy family?" Randy asked.

"NO!" Twisted twitched in disgust. "I'm gonna PUKE!"

Randy tossed him a barf bag, then faced Dazzlessence. "I feel dazzling for the first time in a long time. Maybe we can sheriff this moon together?"

"Um," Dazz said.

"Think about it," Randy said.

"Maybe on holiday weekends?"

"I love the holidays."

Sleepy did three jumping jacks to gather his energy. Then, he pointed his horn at the stars and fired. Top hats and canes rained from the sky. A top hat landed on Twisted's horn. Next, a cane knocked him in the head. It was too much. In a rage, he began to twist. *Faster, faster, faster!*

"I'LL BE BACK YOU DANCY, FEELY MORONS!" he screamed, twisting off the moon.

Hanazuki, Lavender, and their friends didn't even bother to wave goodbye. Instead, they launched into a giant dance number behind Dazz and Randy, who were dressed in matching sequined blazers. They double buffaloed and bombershayed. They jump-clipped and cramp-rolled. They paradiddled and waltz-clogged. Meanwhile, the Hotaru framed them, lighting them up like a marquee.

As Dazzlessence and Randy harmonized the final note of the number, Lavender squeezed between Hanazuki and Kiazuki for a hug. The three of them grinned at the inspirational lavender Treasure Trees, sprouted just in time for the curtain call.

CHAPTER TEN

CURTAIN UP

I t was three weeks later when Hanazuki walked past the newly sprouted Treasure Tree groves of all colors and arrived at the lavender one where her friends had built a performance studio. During its construction, she'd been moon-hopping, networking, and attending theater-management conferences in preparation for her new role as artistic director. Shaking with excitement, she rang the doorbell. *Ding-dong-dong!*

Dazzlessence opened the door, wearing a sequined security guard uniform. "*Welcome to Sparkle Together Studios,*" he sang, handing her an ARTISTIC DIRECTOR pin.

Hanazuki beamed, taking in the GRAND OPENING banner hanging above the door. The velvet ropes leading to the box office. The mirrored signs for the dressing room, concession stand, and stage. "Do I get the full tour?" she asked. "I need the full tour!!!"

Randy, wearing a STUDIO TOUR GUIDE pin, emerged from behind a purple velvet curtain. "Right this way, boss." He led her down a short hallway to the box office, where Maroshi, wearing a COMPANY MANAGER SLASH MARKETING DIRECTOR pin, was distributing flyers. "Super-rad first talent show tonight at eight, man," he said to Doughy Bunington. "Check it out."

"I'll already be here working the concession stand," Doughy told him, pointing to his BUY TREATS FROM ME pin, "but I'll try to catch the end. Popcorn pastries. It's a very important thing."

"Butter and corn, man. The magical pairing."

Randy plucked a flyer from Maroshi's hands and showed it to Hanazuki. She nodded with approval—it was bright and eye-catching and clearly presented all the necessary information. "So you did end up booking Hoshi to perform tonight?" she asked.

Maroshi nodded. "He's got a *Moonhouse* model shoot this afternoon, but now that he's got his own spaceboard, he says he'll be able to get here right on time. As long as we provide a neti pot, which is a nostril-cleaning kettle. And a bowl of chewy candy—only magenta colored. Plus, throat-coat tea and a tabletop Zen garden. The expensive kind."

"*Of course*," Hanazuki joked. "Anything for the galaxy's most modest Moonflower."

"Miyumi is performing, too," Maroshi said. "She's in her dressing room, warming up 'fab-tastically.' And eating her microphone."

"Um."

"Don't worry—it's chocolate."

Just then, Hanazuki heard a whoosh and turned around. Kiyoshi, wearing a HOUSE MANAGER pin, was waving a golden ticket out the box office window. "Are you looking to score free entry?" he asked.

"I'll absolutely take my comp," Hanazuki replied with a smirk, examining the studio imprint on the ticket's foil. "Fancy! So, what else is on tap tonight? Other than Hoshi and Miyumi's acts?"

Kiyoshi smiled. "Oh, we've got a whole bunch of moon creatures and Moonflowers signed up to workshop their newest material or perform just for fun. Kiazuki has the lineup."

"Ah, I can't wait!" Hanazuki caught sight of Randy waving her through a lavender curtain, so she tucked the ticket in her pocket and followed him backstage. Kiazuki was there, wearing a TECHNICAL DIRECTOR pin and hanging the show's running order in the wings. "Hiya, Kiazuki! Can I see?"

"Sure," she said, stepping aside. "All the Hemka opted to perform, but they also work as the stagehands. Lavender's working triple duty as the stage manager, stunt director, and Gymnastics Act Break performer."

"Of course he is," Hanazuki said with a proud smile. "By the way, are you gearing up for our joint spa day tomorrow?"

"Duh. It could not come any sooner. The two of us deserve a twenty-four-hour staycation."

"Yes! Exactly! I'll fetch us the first round of fruit drinks if you get the second."

"I'll get the second if you get the third."

"Deal," Hanazuki said, giving her Moonflower sister a shake.

"Aw, cute mccutes! Did someone say 'spa day?'" Miyumi asked, suddenly sauntering into the conversation with half a chocolate microphone in one hand and BB in the other. "I'd say tell me when and we'll sync calendars, but my whole body is on vocal rest and spa treatment sounds exhausting. Anyway, you do you. That's what I do. I do me. Mi-yu-mi. Wish me luck."

Before Hanazuki could wish her luck, let alone

get a word in, Miyumi was flouncing back to her dressing room. Hanazuki and Kiazuki shared a grin. "Who's emceeing tonight?" Hanazuki asked.

Kiazuki pointed at Sleepy Unicorn, who was fast asleep on a feather cot protruding from a dressing room. "Let's see if he wakes up. Otherwise, Dazz and Randy will cohost."

"He's got ten minutes," Randy grumbled. Then to Hanazuki, "You're all set to say a few words to the audience? About the studio's premier season?"

"Absolutely," Hanazuki said. "I'm gonna take a seat in the audience and look over my speech." Sitting in the third row, she unfolded a piece of paper from her pocket. She skimmed her own words, welcoming the Moonflowers from all over the galaxy and introducing some of the incredible acts making their debut. Lavender would be workshopping a one-Hemka show. Dazz and Randy would be releasing their Jones

Brothers album of dance music, *It's About Shine*. Sleepy Unicorn would be experimenting with performance nap. Hanazuki officially had her hands full with the best part of the job—directing all the wonderful art her friends were about to make waves with on her moon and beyond.

Somehow, without a peep, Lavender had curled up in the seat beside her. "Soo za chee ra?" he whispered.

"I hear everybody perfectly," Hanazuki assured him.

Lavender nodded, satisfied, then waved Purple Hemka to the left as he laid glow tape on the stage.

Hanazuki felt her stomach flip with pride. "Without you, Lav, none of this would be possible," she told him. "Seriously, you find solutions that change everyone's lives for the better. I don't know how you do it."

Lavender blushed and threw his ears over his face.

"Oh, come on! Don't go all shy on me now," Hanazuki joked.

Lavender laid his ear over Hanazuki's heart. "Zee ma inspa," he said. "Ya ya?"

"I do see." Hanazuki's eyes pooled up. She wrapped her arms around him and gave him a giant, giggly squeeze. "We're each other's inspiration, and that's what bonds us together."

Just when her tears spilled over, Hoshi arrived in head-to-toe faux fur and a new mullet haircut. "I'm heeeere!" he called out, waving a flag with his Hotaru on it. "Are we getting this show started or what?"

Lavender winked at Hanazuki, then did a double back handspring offstage, landing in an upside-down ear-split.

"The house is now open!" called Kiyoshi. "Welcome to the studio's opening night! If you're performing in the second act, please take a seat in the audience and enjoy the show!"

Hanazuki followed Lavender backstage as

Moonflowers and their alterlings from all over the galaxy filtered in. Peeking out from behind the stage curtain, she could see a Moonflower with green dreadlocks. A Moonflower on stilts. A Moonflower wearing layers of armor. It was like Lunaverse's Got Talent all over again! Except without the scam.

Five minutes later, the house lights dimmed, the spotlight circled the stage, and the music swelled. Hanazuki stared at her speech, psyching herself up, when she felt dozens of supportive hands pat her back. Her friends' words of encouragement—"Break a leg!" and "We all sparkle together!"—swirled all around her. She exchanged one last thumbs-up with Lavender and, for the first time feeling like she could do just about anything in the lunaverse, the curtain began to rise.

About the Author

Stacy Davidowitz is an author, playwright, and screenwriter based in Manhattan. Her book babies include *Camp Rolling Hills*, *Crossing Over*, *Breakout!,* and *Freefall*. When she's not writing, you can find her teaching creative writing and theater, running long distances, and singing show tunes. Visit her at stacydavidowitz.com.

About the Illustrator

Victoria Ying is a rare native Angeleno. She started her career in the arts by falling in love with comic books. This eventually turned into a career working in animation. She loves Japanese curry, putting things in her online shopping cart and taking them out again, and hanging out with her dopey dog. Her book credits include *Meow!*; *Not Quite Black and White*; *Lost and Found, What's That Sound?*; and *Unicorn Magic*.

Collect All 3!

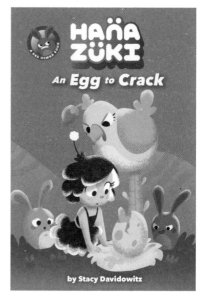